P9-APB-244

Dear Reader:

LOVESWEPT celebrates heroes, those irresistible men who sweep us off our feet, who tantalize us with whispered endearments, and who challenge us with their teasing humor and hidden vulnerability. Whether they're sexy roughnecks or dashing sophisticates, dark and dangerous or blond and brash, these men are heartthrobs, the kind no woman can get enough of. And now, just in time for Valentine's Day, all six books in this month's line-up have truly special covers that feature only these gorgeous heartthrobs. HEARTTHROBS—heroes who'll leave you spellbound as only real men can, in six fabulous new romances by only the best in the genre.

Don't miss any of our HEARTTHROBS this month

There's no better way to celebrate the most romantic day of the year than to cuddle up with all six LOVESWEPT HEARTTHROBS!

With best wishes,

Nita Taublib

Nita Taublib
Associate Publisher/LOVESWEPT

WHAT ARE *LOVESWEPT* ROMANCES?

They are stories of true romance and touching emotion. We believe those two very important ingredients are constants in our highly sensual and very believable stories in the *LOVESWEPT* line. Our goal is to give you, the reader, stories of consistently high quality that may sometimes make you laugh, sometimes make you cry, but are always fresh and creative and contain many delightful surprises within their pages.

Most romance fans read an enormous number of books. Those they truly love, they keep. Others may be traded with friends and soon forgotten. We hope that each *LOVESWEPT* romance will be a treasure—a "keeper." We will always try to publish

LOVE STORIES YOU'LL NEVER FORGET
BY AUTHORS YOU'LL ALWAYS REMEMBER

The Editors

Loveswept ® 532

Tami Hoag
Taken by Storm

BANTAM BOOKS
NEW YORK · TORONTO · LONDON · SYDNEY · AUCKLAND

TAKEN BY STORM

A Bantam Book / March 1992

*If you would be interested in receiving protective vinyl
covers for your Loveswept books, please write to this address
for information:*

Loveswept
Bantam Books
P.O. Box 985
Hicksville, NY 11802

ISBN 0-553-44164-7

Published simultaneously in the United States and Canada

PRINTED IN THE UNITED STATES OF AMERICA

OPM   0 9 8 7 6 5 4 3 2 1

Prologue

I want to marry her.

S. T. Dalton opened his eyes and looked around the bedroom of his apartment. It could have been a hotel room for all its warmth and personality. He was alone in his big bed as he had been every morning for the past year and half, ever since he'd been traded from Minnesota to Kansas City. But today seemed different, the world a strange place he didn't quite feel comfortable in. Yesterday he had been a celebrity, the venerable backup quarterback who had stepped in and saved the season for the Chiefs; "Storm" Dalton, the man who had once been described as having legs like lightning and an arm like a thunderbolt. Today he was just plain S. T. Dalton, an ex-cowboy from Muleshoe, Montana. Today he was retired.

The process of getting out of bed was a long and painful one, requiring the manipulation of joints that had taken too many years of pounding. His knees were bad, and his back was chronically stiff on arising. He had a bum shoulder and an ankle that could predict rain with one-hundred-percent accuracy. Once all the parts got warmed up they still worked reasonably well. He was thankful for that.

Under the watchful eye of his German shepherd he

pulled on a wrinkled pair of jeans, zipped them, shuffled across the room, and stood leaning against the dresser, staring himself down in the mirror. He was thirty-six years old. Women and advertising people liked his face, but he personally thought he looked like forty miles of a bad highway if he wasn't smiling. He scratched a hand through his black hair and let out a long breath.

Yesterday he had closed the door on the career that had consumed his life from high school. It was a strange sensation. He felt at once old and reborn. The rest of his life stretched before him like a long dusty road.

He knew exactly what he wanted to do with it. Even as he stood there the last piece of the puzzle fell into place and he finally saw the whole picture with absolute clarity. It had taken him years to get there and he'd taken plenty of wrong turns along the way, but he'd finally arrived at the crossroads and he knew exactly which way to go. The sense of peace and purpose that came with that realization was amazing. The last of the old ghosts drifted away. The last of the old fears vanished.

He wanted to marry Julia McCarver.

His gaze fell to the curling photographs tucked into the frame of the mirror, the only personal things in the apartment. He focused on the progression of Julia: a gangly teenager showing the promise of beauty and the uncertainty of youth; a young woman graduating from college, dark eyes full of enthusiasm for the future; a woman in faded jeans, T-shirt, and leather jacket, long red hair in disarray, her expression pensive, a grown beauty still unimpressed by her own looks.

He'd known her for years. He'd loved her forever. He'd hurt her more than once. He'd taken her love and hoarded it, cherished it, immersed himself in it, but every time the subject of commitment had come up he'd headed south, so afraid he'd blow it that he blew it every time.

How many years had he wasted worrying he was his father's son, that deep down he was just as no-account and unreliable as old Bud? How much time had he wasted running from the one person in the world who was his soul mate? It didn't matter. Those years were behind him. It was time to get on with the rest of his life. Now all he had to do was convince the lady in the photographs that she had a permanent place in that life, just as she had always had a permanent place in his heart.

"Well, Bingo," he drawled, turning a wry smile on the enormous dog that had settled himself in the middle of the bed. "We'd better get a move on. We've got our work cut out for us."

One

"I've decided to get married."

Julia McCarver looked at her roommate over the heavy black rims of her reading glasses. Liz Costa sat in an overstuffed smoke-blue chair, her tiny feet propped on the bleached-pine coffee table as she painted her toenails an alarming shade of red. She looked as unconcerned as if she had just announced she had decided to eat toast for breakfast.

Absently Julia licked a fingertip and turned the page of her medical journal without looking at it. After a long moment of puzzled silence she said, "But you're not dating anyone."

"A mere formality."

"Kind of a major formality, I'd say."

Liz shook her head, sending her fashionable black bob swinging artfully around the circle of her face. "There are plenty of men out there. I just have to apply myself," she said, a hint of a Puerto Rican accent flavoring her words like a dash of hot pepper. "The time is right. If I send out the proper signals, the man of my destiny will be drawn to me. I read that in *Vogue.*"

"Yeah, that's where I get all my life's wisdom," Julia drawled, rearranging her long legs on the couch. "Is that what brought on this sudden change of heart? An article in a fashion magazine? What happened to Liz Costa, liberated independent businesswoman?"

Liz waved a dainty, elegantly manicured hand. "That was in the eighties, the Me Decade. Get with the program, Julia. This is the nineties, the age of New Traditionalism. Romance is in."

"Well, that settles it. We wouldn't want you to be unfashionable."

Liz sat back and wiggled her toes as the doorbell rang. "My polish is wet," she said as Julia unfolded herself from the sofa and headed for the foyer. "I won't come to the door unless it's Kevin Costner."

"It's probably the man of your destiny being drawn to you."

"Could be. I've been sending out signals since Thursday."

Julia trudged up the three steps to the entrance hall and swung the door open. Her heart stopped dead. She stood on the threshold, stunned, clutching the doorknob for support as she stared at the man who had first captured her heart as a teenager, the man who had broken her heart on three separate occasions, the man she had vowed never to let anywhere near her heart again: S. T. Dalton.

She had told herself she would never see him again, that she never *wanted* to see him again. But there he was, in the flesh, six feet two inches of lean, muscular cowboy with shoulders as wide as the Parthenon. Despite the fact that he had probably made more money than God during his years in football, he still dressed like a ranch hand—battered boots, faded jeans that molded every masculine inch of his lower body, a chambray shirt with the sleeves rolled back. He held a dusty, disreputable-looking black Stetson in one hand as he stood before her, his face set in uncharacteristically stern lines of concentration.

He had aged a bit since she'd last seen him,

although he wore the lines beside his eyes and mouth as comfortably as a model wears an Armani suit. At thirty-six he looked as if he was just coming into the prime of desirability. Then again, S.T. had always looked that way—ripe for trouble, impossibly sexy, handsome in a way that had nothing to do with the arrangement of his features. In fact, his cheekbones were a little too high, his chin a little too long, and his nose had been broken at least once, but none of that mattered because he radiated magnetism. He was a natural generator of sex appeal. It thrummed in the air around him and burned in his blue eyes, and Julia had yet to meet the woman who was immune to it.

She wasn't immune to it, much to her consternation. She hadn't been immune to it at sixteen or at twenty or at thirty-two. Storm Dalton's charm was like a virus in her blood. Even now she felt a flash of fever. She lifted a hand to her forehead to check her temperature and hit herself in the face with the magazine she'd been reading, knocking her glasses askew.

"Well, if it isn't the Lone Stranger," she said dryly, trying to cover her shock with sarcasm.

S.T. gave her a hesitant, lopsided smile. He was shaking inside. He'd rehearsed this moment in his head a thousand times as he'd driven north from Kansas City. He'd pictured Julia standing in the doorway looking implacable, pictured himself saying some magical phrase that would erase all the hurt he'd dealt her in the past. But now that the time was at hand, he couldn't remember any of the magic words. Now that he actually saw her standing there, he couldn't get himself past the fear that nothing he could say or do would get her to take him back. He could feel their past rise up between them like a wall.

"It's mighty good to see you, Legs," he drawled softly in the smoke-edged voice that had driven more than one sane woman wild with desire. For Julia it conjured images of whiskey and smoke and rumpled sheets. The fact of the matter was he'd gotten clothes-lined by a two-hundred-pound tackle in the tenth grade and had sounded this way ever since, but knowing that didn't dilute the effect a bit.

Julia scowled at him. "I'd say the same if it were true, but frankly I'd rather open my door and find a cobra on the step. At least I'd know that's a snake instead of just acting like one."

S.T. winced. "That hurt."

Julia shook her head, narrowing her eyes with contempt. "You don't know the meaning of the word."

"Yes, I do."

"Sorry," Julia sneered, unmoved by his ability to look sincere. "I know you think you have all the monosyllables memorized, but that one has managed to escape your grasp."

S.T. took it on the chin. He knew he deserved her cutting remarks. Hell, he probably deserved to have her cut him up with a dull, rusty knife and feed him to stray dogs, but he had come here to change all that if he could. This woman was his destiny, the woman he'd loved and left and loved still. The woman glaring at him with all the ferocity of an angry tigress.

He stared at her and saw the same wide-eyed girl he'd known back in Muleshoe, an overgrown tomboy who had blossomed into a swan and couldn't quite get used to it. The glasses she wore looked as if they belonged to Buddy Holly. Her faded navy-blue T-shirt hung shapelessly to her hips and proclaimed in peeling white letters TRAUMA NURSES DO IT STAT. A baggy pair of men's boxer shorts revealed a mile of shapely female leg. Her waist-long mane tumbled in wild disarray all around her. She didn't wear a hint of makeup. Despite all of that, she was gorgeous.

S.T. tilted his head a little to one side, spilling a few strands of black hair across his broad forehead. His eyebrows lifted hopefully. "Could I come in?"

"No."

Julia stepped back and closed the door on the biggest part of her past. She left the tiny front hall in a daze, walked back across the living room and resettled herself on the sofa, curling her legs beneath her once more. Her heart was pounding, her ears were ringing. She felt hot and cold at once. The virus was back. Stormitis. The man was no different than a case of malaria, recurring when she least expected it, driving her out of her mind. Forget curing the common cold. If someone could come up with a vaccine to fight the effect of Storm Dalton on women, *that* would be worth something.

Liz glanced up from her second coat of polish, only vaguely curious. "Salesman?"

Julia's wide mouth twisted, caught between a smile and a grimace. "I didn't want any."

"What was he selling?"

"Horse manure."

Liz made a face. "Odd thing to be selling door-to-door."

Julia pretended to turn her attention back to the article she'd been reading before the doorbell had rung, but somehow obstructed bowels didn't grab her interest at the moment. As a visual image they couldn't hold a candle to S. T. Dalton. Damn, but he looked good. It should have been illegal for the man to wear tight jeans.

"Was he *that* cute?" Liz asked slyly.

A guilty flush crept under her skin as Julia glanced up at her friend. Liz was regarding her with her black eyes narrowed to slits, full lips pursed. Liz had an unerring eye for detail, which made her very successful as the manager of one of the trendiest boutiques in Minneapolis. It also made her uncomfortably insightful as a friend.

"You look the way I felt the time I met Mel Gibson in New York," she said. "Hot, cold, dizzy, weak."

"Sounds like the flu."

"Oh, no," Liz said, adopting her Look of Great

Wisdom. She stuck the brush back into the polish bottle so she could talk with her hands. "It was hormones. Raging hormones. The kind of hormones that race through your veins like wild horses. The kind of hormones that give off enough heat to thaw the polar ice caps. The kind of hormones that make you want to grab a man by the—"

"Enough!" Julia exclaimed, throwing her hands up in a gesture of finality. "Enough with the hormones already! I don't have hormones. My hormones are in remission."

Liz lifted one artfully plucked brow. "Boring Bob will be crushed to hear it."

"Bob—?" Julia cut herself short as panic grabbed her by the throat. Robert. She had forgotten Robert! One look at S. T. Dalton and her whole world was turned upside down. She had even forgotten her relationship with the most eligible plastic surgeon in the metro area. A sense of impending doom weighed down on her like a stone.

Why had S. T. Dalton come back? What did he want from her? They hadn't had any contact in over a year. Not since the Vikings had traded him to Kansas City for a second-string wide receiver and a third-round draft pick. He had walked out of her life then—for the third time—and she hadn't heard from him since. Now he'd turned up again, like the proverbial bad penny.

The doorbell rang with a loud, insistent buzz that nearly catapulted Julia to the ceiling. Liz looked on in amused silence as she proceeded to fall all over herself in an attempt to get to the door.

"That must be some kind of horse manure."

Julia made no comment as she crossed to the foyer. She swung the door open and glared at the man standing on the step. "What do you want?"

"You," S.T. said with a sweet, lazy smile. He didn't really expect to charm her that easily. In fact, he didn't expect she would be charmed at all, but he couldn't help himself. Charm was a reflex for him, a defense, an all-purpose tool. He had learned at an early age to wield it with skill in situations where all else failed.

His answer had the same effect on Julia as a hammer blow between the eyes. She felt her head swim and her knees go weak, but she hardened herself. She would not think of the past they shared. She would absolutely not think of the sex they had shared. She wouldn't let herself remember how he looked naked—the granite-hard chest and washboard stomach, the horseman's thighs and a backside that was— She would *not* let him charm his way into her house or her bed or her heart, and that was that. Storm Dalton had done all the damage to her life he was ever going to do.

She regarded him with her steeliest head-nurse look. "Sorry, I'm not in the market for any bastards today. I've had all I can stand for this lifetime, thanks."

"How about apologies?" he asked sincerely.

"I'm full up on apologies. Call again when hell freezes over."

She started to shut the door, but S.T. reacted with all the finesse of the athlete he was. He grabbed her by one wrist, pulled her out onto the wide front step, and shut the door behind her, all in one fluid motion that left Julia breathless. He blocked her route to the door by bracing a hand against the wall. She turned to bolt the other way, but he blocked that path, too, and she found herself virtually corralled against the wall of her house.

"What do you think you're doing?" she demanded indignantly. With S.T. leaning toward her they were at eye level. Definitely the wrong place to be. His brilliant blue eyes looked into hers with a stubborn intensity that sent shivers through her.

"I'm apologizing," he murmured. "I reckon it could take all day, considering what I've got to make up for, so I hope you're comfortable."

"I don't want to hear it."

"Maybe you don't, but I need to say it. I'm sorry I hurt you, baby."

Julia glanced away, barely resisting the urge to fan herself with her hand. Her body temperature had jumped twenty degrees. She could still feel the laser beam of his gaze lingering on her face. Tingles ran over her from head to toe, concentrating in all her most sensitive parts. It was amazing, really, that she could still react to him this way. He had become the prime example of everything she loathed in a man and yet a part of her was still attracted to him. It made her furious and terrified.

"Uh-huh," she said, willing her anger to override her instinctive response to him. "You're sorry for leaving for Kansas City while I was on duty at the hospital, or are we going back to the time you dumped me before your first pro training camp?"

"All of it. For every rotten thing I ever did."

"What do you want from me, S.T.? Forgiveness? Absolution?"

His jaw tightened, but his gaze didn't waver. She'd never seen him so serious. "Another chance," he said simply.

Julia's heart jolted into a weird arrhythmia, as if she'd been given an electric shock. She stared at him for a long second before her temper rushed to her rescue.

"Of all the colossal nerve!" She ducked under his arm and came up pacing the width of the tiny porch, shaking her head. "I've got news for you, Seth Thomas Dalton. I don't care how sorry you are. I don't care if you mean to take a pledge of celibacy and shave your head bald to prove it. I don't want to hear your 'let's start over' bull hooey. You're out of my life. Do you understand me? Have I made myself perfectly clear? You're gone, finished, *finito*, out of here."

S.T. stood with his hands on his hips, one leg

cocked, hat tipped back on his head, his face grave. "You've got every right to be mad at me."

"Mad?" Julia nearly choked on the word. She could feel her blood pressure shooting up ten points. A red haze swam before her eyes. "Mad doesn't begin to cover it! You think you can just waltz back in here and sweep me off my feet?"

"No."

She went on, impervious to his answer. "Think again, you boneheaded, dirt-for-brains cowboy. I'll show you mad."

Her fury came exploding to the surface, blasting away common sense and self-control. She looked around wildly, hoping to find something she could throw at him with gusto. Her gaze landed on a foot-tall painted-plaster gnome beside the front door. Without giving it a second thought, she snatched it up and rushed S.T. with it, giving a warrior's cry as she raised the gnome high over her head.

S.T. dodged her at the last second, hopping down off the front step and onto the yard. Julia's momentum carried her past him. She pulled up and swung around, staggering slightly sideways as the weight of the gnome threw her off balance. Huffing and puffing like a wild bull, she charged back across the lawn.

"Now, Julia," S.T. said, raising a hand to hold her off as he shuffled backward. "Can't we talk this over like adults?"

"I'd love to, but I may grow old and die before you become one."

"But that's why I'm here—to let you know I've changed."

"That'll be the day. The only change I'm ever going to see in you is the goose egg on your head after I bop you one with this gnome."

He backed away a step and moved a little to the left, never taking his eyes off Julia as she moved with him. "Now, honey, do you really want to do that out here in front of God and all your neighbors?"

Julia pulled up abruptly and looked around her, gnome still aloft. It was a lovely summer Saturday morning in the Minneapolis suburb of Bloomington. All around them people were watering their lawns, pruning their hedges, watching her make a royal fool of herself. Mrs. Perkins next door was flooding her bird bath as she stared. Gus Thorenson waved at her with his Weed Eater and gave the thumbs-up sign to S.T. Across the street, old Mr. Peabody was sitting on his porch in his wheelchair, ogling her through binoculars. She looked up at the gnome that was grinning down at her. She looked down at the paisley boxer shorts she wore. She looked up at S.T.

"Now I'm *really* going to kill you," she said in a low, tight voice.

She hurled the gnome at him, but he dodged it easily and the plaster dwarf landed on its head in a potentilla shrub. S.T.'s brows pulled together in annoyance.

"Now, that's enough of that," he declared, his good humor vanishing. "I came here to talk to you, Julia, and I'm damn well gonna do it if I have to hog-tie you."

Julia was aware of the momentum of the situation shifting. She was no longer the hunter but the hunted. S.T. took a menacing step toward her and she backed away, trying to watch him and look for something to defend herself with, all at once. The only thing in sight was a giant rawhide bone the neighbor's Great Dane had left in the yard. She scooped it up and brandished it in front of her as if it were a knife.

"Don't come any closer."

S.T.'s lips twitched. She looked ridiculous standing there in her weird getup, waving a dog bone at him, eyes wide behind her Buddy Holly glasses. He had no doubt she would indeed smack him a good one with the bulbous end of the dog bone, but he couldn't work up much apprehension about it. Admiration was the greater part of what he was feeling. Julia was no shrinking violet, no swooning fan. She didn't give a rip how famous he had been or how much money he had made. He couldn't buffalo her. What a woman.

Julia watched him warily as he gave one sharp whistle and his big German shepherd came flying out the open window of the black pickup parked on the street. With a simple hand signal S.T. sent the dog bounding across the lawn, headed straight for her impromptu weapon. Eyes bright with excitement, tongue lolling out the side of his mouth, the dog made a graceful leap, snatched the bone from her hand, and tore around the yard with it, yipping in triumph.

S.T. took advantage of the distraction and made his move. He lunged forward, head down. Julia shrieked as he caught her in the midsection with a shoulder and straightened, lifting her off her feet. She fell over his shoulder like a giant rag doll, derriere up, head down, arms flailing. She tried to kick him, but he banded one arm around her legs.

"Quit!" he ordered as he turned and headed for the sidewalk.

"I will not quit!" Julia said, squirming. He staggered sideways and she managed to knock his hat off, but he didn't release her. "This is a civilized place, Storm Dalton. You can't just cart women off over your shoulder!"

"Yeah, well, I'm doing it."

"I hope you get a hernia."

"That's not very nice."

"Call me strange, but I get crabby when I'm held upside down for any length of time," she snapped, craning her head around and scraping the hair out of her eyes so she could see where he was taking her. They were nearing the front porch of the house. If Liz got a look at her predicament she would never live it down. "Now that you've humiliated me utterly in front of my neighbors, will you please put me down?"

"That all depends," he said, patting her fanny absently. "Are you gonna behave yourself?"

"Yes. Not that you have any understanding of proper behavior," Julia snapped, furious with him and with herself. The feel of his hand against her bottom had set loose a stampede of those wild, raging hormones she supposedly didn't have.

"Oh, I understand it," S.T. drawled. "I just don't always hold to it, that's all."

"No kidding."

He stepped up onto the porch, leaned over and set her on her feet. Julia straightened with as much dignity as she could muster, tugging down the hem of her T-shirt, straightening her glasses, trying in vain to restore some order to her hair.

"Are we going inside now to talk?" he asked, his expression strongly advising she say yes.

"There's nothing for us to talk about, S.T.," she said quietly, crossing her arms in front of her. She felt naked, vulnerable, as if nerves that had finally stopped hurting had suddenly been exposed again. Dammit, why did he have to keep coming back to her? How could she look at him and still feel that tug of attraction in her middle? Well, it didn't matter, because the Storm Dalton chapter of her life was over, and that was all there was to it.

"You're wrong, Julia," he said, his gaze rock-steady and as blue as the sea. "There's plenty for us to talk about. I want to make up for all the mistakes I've made in the past. I want us to be friends again. I want us to get married."

Two

"Married?" The word escaped Julia on what she thought must be her dying breath. Married? Storm Dalton? The man had an allergy to commitment that was so acute he should have worn a Medic Alert bracelet for it. And *he* was suggesting marriage? Impossible.

"I'm sorry," she said, giving him a skeptical look that knitted her brows together. "I had to have misunderstood. I thought you said you wanted us to get married."

S.T. shuffled his boots against the concrete. He had never been so nervous in his life. Facing the goal line, waiting for the snap on third and long with nine seconds to go in the league championship game with his team down by six points, had been a breeze compared to this. The antiperspirant he endorsed gave out abruptly.

He hadn't meant to blurt out a proposal. He had meant to court her and woo her first, to let her see that he wasn't the same man who'd run away from her before. Of course Julia would be wary of him; he'd let her down more times than he cared to count. But those days were over for good, and he wanted her to know it. The proposal had just seemed like the thing to do once he had confronted her. Lay his cards on the table. Be up-front and honest. He was by nature a gambler and a risk taker, a man who went after what he wanted. He wanted the woman who was standing in front of him now, looking at him as if he had suddenly sprouted a second nose. It seemed only fair to let her know.

"Married?" she questioned. "You said *married*. M-A-R-R-I-E-D. The dreaded *M* word. I heard it come out of your mouth."

S.T. sucked in a short, hard breath. Beads of sweat popped out on his forehead. "Yep."

"Married."

"Married."

Conflicting emotions whirled through Julia like a tornado. There had been a time not so long ago when she would have given anything to hear that word come from S.T.'s lips. There was a part of her heart that had longed to hear it way back when she had been sixteen and in love for the first time, falling like a rock for her cousin's best friend; when she had been twenty and had watched him drive off for his first pro training camp, dragging her heart behind him; when she had been thirty-two and almost convinced he had grown up at last. But it was too late now.

"You're a day late and a dollar short, cowboy," she said with a bittersweet mixture of anger and regret. "I've already got a fiancé."

S.T. looked as if she'd hit him in the head with a brick. He swayed a little. The German shepherd looked up at him with concern and whined. Ignoring the dog, who held the Stetson in his mouth, S.T. stumbled off the porch and onto the lawn. He heaved a sigh, ran a hand through his hair, then shook his head, sending strands of black tumbling down across his forehead.

"Damn, Legs," he muttered as he turned toward

her looking hurt and confused. "You went and got engaged? To another man?"

"No, to an orangutan," Julia said sarcastically. "Of course to another man. What did you think—that I'd just hang around and wait for you to come wandering back again? I have better things to do with my life than to wait on you."

S.T.'s dark brows pulled together. He jammed his hands at the waist of his jeans and concentrated all his energies into scowling. Damnation. He hadn't taken this possibility into account at all. Another man! Hell!

He knew Julia was capable of attracting other men. Shoot, there probably wasn't a red-blooded man alive who *wouldn't* be attracted to her. But he had always seen her as *his*. From the first there had been something between them, a bond, a kinship of spirit. They understood each other. And she was going to turn her back on that and marry some other man.

The idea made him wild with jealousy, whether he had the right to feel that way or not. He wanted the fiancé to materialize so he could whup the living daylights out of him, just to take the edge off his temper. But he doubted the man would be that accommodating, and he knew for a fact Julia wouldn't be amused. She would probably find that dog bone and make mincemeat of him.

He swore and kicked at a dandelion. What the hell was he supposed to do now? She was his future, his destiny. She was engaged to another man. His heart sank. Then his gaze homed in on Julia's left hand, looking for some tangible evidence of this nameless, faceless son of a bucket who had rustled away his woman. There wasn't any. All he saw were long fingers and short unpolished nails. He jerked his head up, his blue eyes burning as bright as a zealot's.

"I don't see a ring."

Julia felt her cheeks heat a little under the intensity of his gaze. She rubbed the back of her hand against her leg, wishing she had given in the last time Robert had suggested they hunt for a suitable diamond. "Well, we haven't gotten around to picking one out yet, but—"

"When's the wedding?"

"The date isn't set, but—"

S.T. shook a finger at her. A great big bandit's grin stretched across his face—that old familiar Storm Dalton grin that had been nowhere in evidence to this point, wide and wicked, brimming with mischief. He hopped back onto the wide front step and shuffled toward Julia. Julia took one wary step back, and then another, then smacked the back of her head against the side of the house. S.T. shuffled closer, looking like a gambler who'd just hit on a sure thing.

"There's no ring, there's no date, there's no engagement," he said.

Julia narrowed her eyes. "Are you calling me a liar?"

"No, ma'am. I'm calling you a free woman. To use an old hunting expression—meat's not meat till it's in the pan."

"What a flattering comparison."

S.T. ignored her sarcasm. "I don't think I'd let a little thing like an engagement ring stop me, anyway. I mean, it's one thing to steal another man's wife—I draw the line there—"

"I'm glad to know you draw it somewhere—"

"You don't steal another man's horse, you don't steal another man's cattle, you don't kick his dog, and you don't steal his wife," he said, clarifying his personal code of honor. "But this is something else altogether."

Julia tried unsuccessfully to swallow the sudden knot of apprehension that lodged in her throat like a rock. "You stop right there, S.T.," she warned, holding up a hand, hoping to halt his advance without actually having to touch him. "He asked me and I accepted. That makes me engaged."

"Not in my book, it doesn't."

"Well, tough. I don't live my life by *The World According to Storm Dalton*."

"You're name's still McCarver. You're fair game, Legs," he said, that lazy smile curling the corners of his wide mouth as he leaned a little closer.

Julia frowned, pressing back against the wall. "I'm no game at all," she whispered. "I played with you before and lost. I'm not playing again."

Her words ironed his smile into a grim straight line. What she saw behind that burning blue gaze might have been regret, but she told herself it didn't make any difference. She knew he had never set out to hurt her. He wasn't a bad man, just a tough one to tame. Julia knew why he was the way he was, she knew everything there was to know about him, but that didn't make any difference either. What it all boiled down to was that she couldn't trust him not to break her heart again. It was as simple as that.

"I'm not playing again, S.T.," she murmured.

"I know I've hurt you, baby," he said softly, leaning a little closer still. "I'd give anything to be able to go back and undo that, but I can't. All I can do is show you I've changed."

"Nothing's changed," Julia insisted. "You've just retired from football. You're at another crossroads. Time to come back to good old reliable Julia for another little fling. Not this time, S.T. I was your transition from college ball to pro ball, from first string to backup. I won't be your transition from football to whatever. I won't do it again."

"I know I don't deserve another chance," he said, determination flashing like steel in his gaze. "I don't deserve one, but I'm taking one."

"Oh, no, you're not," Julia declared, stubbornly. "There's somebody else. Get that through your thick head, cowboy."

"It's not my head you should be worried about. I'm

hearing you just fine. It's my heart that isn't listening. See?"

He took hold of the hand she had been trying to ward him off with and pressed it to his chest. Julia could have cried. She was touching him. Oh God, *now* she was in trouble. She could feel his heart beat. His chest was warm and hard beneath her palm. She had seen it bare so many times, the image was permanently branded on her brain—perfectly carved pectoral muscles, a light dusting of silky black hair, a short crooked scar from a tangle with a wild cow up in the high pasture back of Bear Woods. Memories involving that chest came forth in a montage of captured moments, most of them erotic. Heat swept through her as one particular image came back to her—the two of them lying naked on a bed of grass and wildflowers, her hand pressed to his chest, his low, rough voice murmuring, "My heart is your heart. . . ."

"You can tell my head anything you want," he said in that same hoarse, husky voice that caressed her nerve endings like velvet. "But you can't tell my heart it's the same between you and him as it was between you and me. You can't tell my heart it's the same when you're in bed with him or that it's the same when he kisses you.

"Remember what it was like, Julia? Soft, slow, deep, wet kisses that lasted half the night." He gave the seductive words a moment to sink in, then leaned a little closer and whispered, "Maybe I ought to refresh your memory."

Julia felt mesmerized as she stared at his mouth. She meant to shake her head, but she couldn't seem to do it. She meant to say no, but she never got any further than forming the shape of the word with her lips. Then S.T.'s mouth was on hers, and the orderly world she had painstakingly created in the past eighteen months was blown to smithereens. It was like a supernova—brilliant colors, a violent energy bursting from within, incredible heat. People could say what they wanted about his ability to throw the ball long, but nobody could call S.T. on this. The man could kiss. There wasn't anybody in his league when it came to a lip lock.

He slanted his mouth across hers slowly, reacquainting himself with her, giving her a chance to do the same, as if the memory of his kiss wasn't burned in acid across her soul. She remembered his kiss the way a child remembers her first taste of chocolate, the way an alcoholic remembers the taste of wine. The flavor of it, the texture of it, the effect of it stayed locked in her mind, never too far from the surface no matter how she tried to bury it. And it came rushing up now, drowning her in a heady mix of memory and new sensation that left her head spinning and her glasses steamed.

Julia knew she should have stopped him, but she couldn't bring herself to do it. The sexual magnetism between them was too strong. Even after all this time. Even after all the pain. As if his touch had flipped a switch inside her, her body responded to his. It responded with a will all its own, defying her brain's frantic efforts to put a stop to the proceedings. It seemed as if his touch had opened a gate inside her, letting loose a wild rush of emotions and memories.

Blast and damn, if only she hadn't touched him!

But she had, and now she couldn't seem to stop.

He tasted like peppermints. His lips were firm and warm and mobile. His tongue was lazy and masterful, exploring and enticing her with languid strokes. As her knees started to give way her arms found their way around S.T.'s mile-wide shoulders and she groaned in despair. This was absolutely the last thing she needed—to want him. But as he slid his arms around her and banded her to him, and her body nestled against his, finding all the spots where they fit together perfectly, she couldn't stem the tide of remembered longing. He'd been her first lover and, damn him, he'd been her best lover. Memories like the ones they had made couldn't simply be erased.

If only she hadn't touched him . . .

After what might have been an eternity S.T. lifted his head, slowly, a fraction of an inch at a time, loath to let go of the moment or the woman. His blood was sizzling in his veins. He would have liked nothing better than to sweep Julia up into his arms and carry her to the nearest bedroom, where they could finish this reunion in style, but one look at her face and he knew that wasn't going to happen. The kiss had managed to awaken memories, that was plain enough, but it was also plain that she wasn't exactly happy about the fact.

A cloud of fury came down over her passion-dazed features like a sudden thunderstorm. She hauled back a fist and punched him hard on the arm, then bolted out of his embrace, colliding once again with the side of the house. The scowl that lowered her brows over her eyes and tugged at the corners of those luscious lips was ominous.

"How dare you kiss me like that!" she hissed, glasses slipping down her nose, her hands knotted into white-knuckled fists at her sides.

S.T. cocked a hip and rubbed his arm, pretending puzzlement. "That's the only way I know how. Is there some other way to do it? You could show me. I'm open for new experiences in intimacy."

"I'll give you an intimate experience with my knee if you try that again," Julia growled, working herself into a fine temper.

S.T. shrugged, not contrite in the least. "I didn't hear you complaining while I was kissing you."

"That's not the point."

"It is as far as I'm concerned."

"No. The point is, it's over. You had your chance and you blew it. Three strikes and you're out, cowboy."

"That's a baseball thing, honey," S.T. said, shaking his head. He let a lazy, predatory smile spread over his face as he slowly backed away from her. "Baseball's a boring game. All those boys just standing around waiting for something to happen. It isn't a wonder they make up so many sayings. But there's only one I ever paid any attention to a-tall." He took his Stetson from his dog and set it on his head, tugging down the brim, his eyes locked on Julia's the whole time. "It ain't over till it's over."

"It's over."

"Not by a long shot," he declared. "I'm gonna win you back, Julia. You're the best thing I ever had in my life and I was too scared of blowing it to hang on, but I'm not running anymore. I'm in your life to stay this time. You might as well get used to the idea."

Julia eyed him warily, too busy digesting his words and their implications to come up with a snappy rejoinder.

"Catch you later, Legs," he said, saluting.

"In your dreams, Dalton."

He smiled softly, sweetly, and Julia's heart hopped in her chest. "Every night, baby," he declared. "Every single night."

Julia shoved aside the warm, fuzzy feeling brought on by thoughts of him dreaming about her. She crossed her arms in front of her and fumed instead, as she watched him amble down the sidewalk toward his pickup. Who did he think he was, pronouncing himself back in her life, dismissing her engagement to another man, setting his sights on her as if she were some grand prize to be won? She wanted to run after him and rant at him some more, but there was the possibility she might wind up touching him again, and she had just seen how dangerous that could be.

No more touching. No more anything. She didn't want to see him again or hear that smoky, sexy voice . . . or taste those lips . . . feel that incredible body . . .

"Cute butt," Liz said with feeling. She was standing in the open front door, leaning a shoulder against the frame, her gaze frankly appreciative as she watched S.T. saunter away with a cocky little bounce in his step.

"Butt-head," Julia grumbled. It *was* a cute butt. Tight, round, muscular . . .

Liz gave her a disturbingly speculative look. "Quite the salesman. I'll bet he meets his quotas *every* month. Any man who kissed me that way could sell me anything he wanted."

Julia shot her a horrified look. "You were watching?"

Liz shrugged it off. "Mrs. Perkins called and told me you were going loco, chasing some cowboy around the yard. It sounded worth smudging my nail polish for. You never get that excited when Dr. Bob comes over."

"That's because Robert is a sane, mature—"

"Boring—"

"—adult, and S. T. Dalton is—is—" She sputtered and her face heated as she choked on a plethora of adjectives.

"Gorgeous," Liz supplied.

"Infuriating!"

Liz arched a brow. "So, did he manage to sell you something?"

"Yeah," Julia said, frowning darkly as S.T. stopped beside his truck to sign an autograph for Gus Thorenson. "A great big load of trouble."

An hour later, Julia was still ranting as she stormed around her bedroom in search of something to tie her hair back with.

"He thinks just because I'm not wearing a ring and

I haven't sent out the invitations yet, I'm fair game. How do you like that?"

Since S.T.'s arrival and departure she had reduced her usually neat sanctuary to a ruin worthy of a tornado. Various articles of nursing whites lay strewn around the room like casualties.

"Well," Liz said slowly, crossing her legs as she sat on the edge of the bed, "those are kind of the traditional signs of being engaged."

Julia's eyes seemed in imminent danger of bursting from their sockets. "I can't believe you'd take his side! You don't even know him!"

Liz rolled her eyes and muttered something in Spanish that sounded as if it might be a prayer for the mentally deficient. "I was merely pointing out that there could be some margin for interpretation here."

Her reasonable explanation was lost on Julia.

"Fair game," she grumbled, digging a broken headband out from under the rubble on her sleek oak dresser. She spun around toward the bed, using the fragment of white plastic like a pointer. "Those were his *exact* words—*fair game*! Like something they'd snare with ropes on *Wild Kingdom*! Like I won't have a choice in the matter if he can manage to lasso me!"

"He's awfully cute," Liz said. "I think a lot of women wouldn't mind having him do anything he wanted with a lasso."

"That's exactly his problem. He has an overblown opinion of his own appeal."

"Yeah," Liz drawled. "I mean really, why would you want him? Just because he's gorgeous and a celebrity and a cowboy and wants to marry you—"

"He doesn't want to marry me," Julia insisted. "S. T. Dalton couldn't spell commitment if you held a gun to his head. He's only here because he's at loose ends, not because he wants to tie the knot. Believe me, I know of what I speak."

"Maybe he really has changed."

Julia shook her head emphatically. "He's just a good ol' boy from Muleshoe, Montana. Everybody's pal. Everybody's hero. Men envy him and women swoon in piles at his feet. And he thinks it's all just swell, that just as long as he's charming and semi-sincere he can get away with anything. Well, not with me. Not anymore."

She started to braid her hair, but her hands were shaking and the long tresses seemed to take on a life of their own, winding around her fingers like tentacles. Her eyes teared up with frustration and she stamped her size-ten sneaker like a thwarted five-year-old.

"Skip it," she snapped, grabbing a new white shoelace from the dresser and tying her mane back in a loose ponytail.

It was a fitting completion for her outfit. She had thrown on clothes without looking at them—a pair of white cotton slacks that were too short for her so she kept the legs rolled up, an oversize white T-shirt with a cartoon on the front of a brain sitting in a beach chair wearing sunglasses and listening to head-phones. County General was too in need of good help to set a strict dress code for the trauma staff.

"You're disgusting," Liz said without malice. "All you need is a pair of big earrings and you could pose for *Glamour.*"

Julia surveyed herself in the mirror. Ever since she had turned sixteen people had been telling her she was beautiful. She didn't really see what the fuss was all about. As far as she was concerned, her mouth was too wide and her eyebrows looked as if they had been drawn on by clowns. She was too tall, her feet were big enough to ski on sans skis, and her hands were like fielder's mitts. She supposed her face had good bone structure, but that hardly seemed anything to get wild about.

She turned away from her reflection and fell into

the upholstered chair beside the bed. A quick check of the enormous man's watch she wore strapped to her wrist told her that if she left for the hospital now she would be only two hours early for the shift she was picking up for another nurse. She propped her feet up on the bed, crossed her arms, and brooded.

"I could cheerfully dismember him with a chain saw for coming back."

"What difference does it make, if you don't want him anymore?"

A simple question, but Julia found it sticking in her throat like a chicken bone. She wasn't hung up on S.T. anymore. She swore she wasn't. What she'd felt when he kissed her was just a little residual lust, a little leftover conditioned response, that was all. She was engaged—despite the lack of physical evidence—to a perfectly nice plastic surgeon. Her life was a bowl of cherries.

Then why did she suddenly feel as if she'd swallowed a pit?

"You don't know S.T.," she said. "I don't trust him any farther than I could throw a sumo wrestler. He's capable of anything."

"Is he capable of making you fall in love with him again?"

"No." The word came out strongly, defensively, but she didn't look at Liz when she said it.

"Then what are you afraid of?"

Julia was silent for a long moment. "I'm not afraid of anything except that I might be late for work."

Instead of sticking to her usual uninteresting path, she took the scenic route, letting her Firebird creep down side streets, through Richfield and into residential Minneapolis, wandering until she came to Lake Harriet. By an unusually benevolent twist of fate she managed to find a parking spot, locked the car, and left it.

The park around the lake was teaming with people, noisy with competing boom boxes, but Julia hardly noticed any of it. She wandered down toward the less populated end of the park to an unoccupied bench under a maple tree. The lake gleamed under the summer sun like a giant sapphire, the sight taking her mind back to a place she hadn't been in years, to another blue lake in a high mountain meadow.

She'd been sixteen and miserable. It was the third summer since her father had uprooted her from Los Angeles and dumped her on her aunt and uncle at their ranch outside Muleshoe, three years since he'd abandoned her for a job with an oil company in the Middle East, three years since her mother had died. During those three years Julia had made hating Montana the driving passion in her life, dedicating herself to it with the zeal of youth. That particular day she had hated it more than ever, because her father had just informed her he had signed on for another three years in the Saudi desert.

She had run out of her uncle's house and hadn't stopped running until she'd seen the blue of the water. It was a mile or more from the house. Her legs were like rubber by the time she got there. When she reached it at last, she hurled herself down on the meadow grass and cried her eyes out, hoping a big rattlesnake would come along and bite her and she would die and then her stingy uncle would have to call clear to the other side of the world to tell her father, and her father would die of guilt over in Saudi Arabia.

She had run out of tears and nearly quit hiccuping when S. T. Dalton came riding up. He almost ran over her, but his horse shied at the last second. He reined in the big bay gelding and scowled down at Julia from beneath the brim of a battered Stetson. He had a black eye, but it didn't do anything to diminish his magnetism.

"What the hell are you doin' down there?" he demanded.

"Whatever the hell I want," she sassed back as she came up on her knees.

Cursing had been one of her favorite forms of rebellion, because it made Aunt Clarisse turn puce. For S.T. it was just a part of his image. For the better part of his adolescence he had been the baddest boy in and around Muleshoe. Everyone knew his mama had run off and his daddy was a drunk who had let S.T. grow up as wild as prairie grass. But his bad-boy days had peaked a couple of years previous when Buck Tanner, the high school football coach, had taken him under his wing. S.T. had gone from the black sheep to the golden boy then, because it had been discovered he could throw a football farther than anyone else in Montana. Most of the bad had been worked out of him, but he still swore as a matter of principle.

"You sure as hell are sassy," he said, swinging down off his horse, a big grin unfurling across his lean face.

"So?"

"So maybe I'd kiss you if your nose wasn't runnin'."

Mortified, Julia stumbled to her feet and turned her back on him, discreetly trying to wipe her nose on the back of her hand. When she turned back toward him, she immediately went on the offensive.

"If you're such hot stuff, who gave you that shiner?"

The smile vanished and he looked away. "My old man."

Julia could have died for asking. She could have choked on the feeling of her great big, ugly, size-ten foot stuffing itself down her throat. She couldn't believe she could be so stupid and live to tell about it.

"I'd'a hit him back," S.T. said, his voice a little huskier than usual, "but I didn't wanna hurt nothing in my throwing hand. I'm going to Colorado State in the fall. Got a scholarship to play ball."

"I know. I'm glad for you, S.T."

"You know?" His teasing grin came back.

Julia smiled, painfully conscious of the fact that her mouth was much too wide. It was like two of Kara Lynn Myer's mouth, and Kara Lynn was head cheerleader and homecoming queen. "Sure I know. Everybody knows that."

S.T. looked down at her, eyes shining. He reached out with his throwing hand and caught a strand of her hair between two fingers. "And does everybody know how pretty you are?"

She shrugged off the compliment and turned to stare at the water. "There's nothing pretty about me," she declared flatly, feeling suddenly twice as big and plain as she thought she was. She felt like one giant lump of homeliness, something no one wanted, something to be hidden away on a ranch in the back of beyond.

S.T.'s voice went soft and smoky. "There's everything pretty about you, Legs." He waggled his eyebrows at her, trying to coax a smile out of her. "I can see right through your clothes, you know."

Julia wished she could have laughed, but to her horror a fresh wave of despair crashed over her without warning, bringing with it a flood tide of tears that welled up in her eyes and clogged her throat. "If I'm so pretty, then how come my dad dumped me here in the middle of nowhere?"

S.T. slid an arm around her and stared across the lake, his eyes as blue as the water. "I don't reckon I know," he murmured. "I'm no expert on why fathers do anything. But it sure as hell wasn't 'cause you're not pretty."

He looked down at her then and Julia felt something forge between them, an unspoken bond, a closeness she hadn't felt with anyone, ever. It was just there, in that moment when she needed so badly to be understood. It was just there.

"You can go ahead and cry on this shirt if you want," he said. "It's mostly clean."

Without a second's hesitation she went into his arms and cried for all she was worth. S.T. held her and patted her back and offered her his handkerchief when she was done. Then he kissed her.

She fell in love with him that day, fell in love with her whole, entire heart. She fell in love the same way she had done everything at sixteen, with every ounce of emotion she had. She had loved him that summer as if her life depended on it. They had shared time and secrets and each other. Then in the fall he had thrown a duffel bag in the cab of his beat-to-death '63 Ford pickup, promised to write, and driven south.

She hadn't seen him again for four years.

Three

"This wouldn't have happened if you hadn't shoved me," the man complained as Julia finished bandaging the gash caused by an irresistible force—the forearm of a man on roller blades—meeting an immovable object—an oak tree. He was in his forties, pale and slim, a desk jockey out for his weekend dose of physical activity. His significant other, an angry-looking brunette built like a wrestler but not as pretty, glared at him from the end of the gurney.

"It wouldn't have happened if you hadn't been gawking at that woman," she growled.

"I wasn't gawking! I glanced. Big deal."

"You would have seen the tree if you hadn't been gawking. Slap a little Spandex around anything big, blond, and Swedish and you go brain-dead!"

Julia secured the end of the bandage and stepped back with a weary sigh. The man climbed down off the cart without so much as a thank you and stalked out of the room, arguing with his lady friend over the inevitability of a man "glancing" at a 38C bosom being contained by a 34B bikini top.

It had been a typical summer Saturday afternoon in the County General emergency room, with a parade of sports-related injuries and weekend warriors with broken bones and torn ligaments, as well as an assortment of beach casualties—sunstroke, cuts, food poisoning, fishing hooks embedded in various body parts. Nothing she hadn't handled a zillion times. It was just that today it required a special effort to keep her mind on her job, and that scared the hell out of her. People in other professions could afford to be distracted on the job occasionally. If she messed up because she was thinking about the way S. T. Dalton's mouth felt on hers, someone could die.

"How goes the battle, beautiful?"

Heart leaping into overdrive at the feel of warm masculine lips on her neck, Julia bolted and wheeled around. "Robert!"

Dr. Robert Christianson tucked his hands into the pockets of his immaculate khaki pants and gave her a quizzical smile. He looked as if he belonged in one of the new bemused-yuppie ads for men's sportswear. "Yes, Robert. Do you have a lot of men kissing your neck and whispering sweet talk to you these days?"

"More than I'd like," Julia grumbled.

Robert's perfect tawny brows drew together over the bridge of his perfect nose. He bore a notable resemblance to Robert Redford, only he was younger and more handsome and quite possibly had an even bigger, whiter smile. He was a nice man, kind, good, reliable. He was also on the verge of questioning her comment when ambulance crews arrived with members of rival soccer teams who were trying their best to exact more damage on each other, even as they were being carried in.

When the ruckus died down at last and there appeared to be a lull in the activities, Julia was allowed to abandon her post for a well-deserved break. She headed for the lounge, half-hoping Robert would be driving back to the suburbs by now. She hadn't recovered from the shock of S.T.'s arrival. She really had no burning desire to spring the news on the man she was supposed to marry.

"Cream, no sugar," Robert said, handing her a cup as she shuffled into the lounge.

She grasped the cup with both hands and took a long, careful sip. The brown sludge didn't even remotely resemble good coffee, but it was imbued with certain life-giving properties essential to the staff of an inner-city emergency room. Even as it burned a path to her stomach, Julia could feel the caffeine being absorbed into her bloodstream. She looked at Robert and managed to mask her disappointment and smile her gratitude.

He looked as out of place in the County General lounge as a prince in a poorhouse. The lounge, affectionately called The Pit by its patrons, hadn't been painted since the Democrats had been in the White House. The walls were a sort of putrid mildew green. The furniture was circa 1950s, eye-burning orange vinyl and big chrome tubes that looked as if they might have come from an exhaust-pipe factory. It was a place to crash between skirmishes with patients. Nothing had been done to encourage anyone to overstay their break time.

"So what drags you off the golf course and down to this level of degradation?" Julia asked as she slid down into a chair and propped her sneakers on the coffee table.

Robert glanced at the sofa with a frown, but didn't sit. Julia wondered if he was more concerned about ruining the crease in his trousers or staining his clothes, then she chided herself for thinking uncharitable thoughts. This was the man she was going to marry. This was the man she loved.

S.T.'s face loomed in her mind like a specter. Something like a claw dug into her stomach. She took another sip of coffee.

"Duty," Robert said. "I'm consulting on a burn victim for Jon Jurgen."

"Gee, you could have lied and said it was me."

He flashed one of his perfect smiles. "I adore you,

beautiful, but I'm afraid in this case you come second to oozing flesh."

"Wow. You sure know how to flatter a girl."

"Quit this dive and come to work for me. I'll flatter you all day, every day."

Julia squeezed her eyes shut and sighed through her teeth. "Robert, I've told you, I have no intention of quitting County General to work for you. I'm needed here."

He heaved an impatient sigh and ran his fingers through his hair. Every blond strand settled perfectly back into place. "I realize you trauma people thrive on excitement. But couldn't you thrive on excitement in a better neighborhood at least? This part of town is so bad, it belongs in New York."

He was right. While most of the Twin Cities area was infused with clean midwestern wholesomeness, the inner city had its share of squalor that seemed to be growing like a cancer every day. The County General ER saw an endless parade of drug addicts, drunks, punks, and victims of violent crimes.

"The world is a dangerous place," Julia said. Her thoughts turned not to the gang violence that seemed constantly on the rise in the city but to the morning's events in quiet Bloomington. Obviously, she wasn't safe even in her own home. Anywhere, at any time, her life could be turned upside down by S. T. Dalton. He could appear out of nowhere and kiss her senseless. . . .

Setting her cup on the table where a dozen others had been abandoned, Julia forced herself to stand up. She looked Robert in the eye and said, "He's back."

"He?" Awareness dawned across his handsome face like the sun. "Oh." He made a doctorly frown. "I see. Well . . ."

Julia scowled. "That's all you can say? *Well?*"

"What do you want me to say?"

"Well . . . *something!*"

She should have known better than to expect some kind of an outburst from him. Robert didn't do outbursts. He didn't do excessive emotion of any kind. He was a calm, rational man. Nothing like S.T. If the situation had been switched around and she had been telling S.T. another man had come sniffing around, he would have been fuming and ranting and making all kinds of macho noises. Not that she wanted that kind of reaction. She was a modern liberated woman, after all.

Still, just a smidgen of jealousy wouldn't have been amiss.

She gave Robert a look of dismay, hoping to jolt a little reaction out of him. "He's claiming he wants to marry me."

The tawny brows rose. It was something, anyway. "But you're going to marry me," he said with calm finality. "So, that settles that."

Julia hit herself in the forehead with the heel of her hand and staggered back a step. "How did you manage to live this long and stay so naive?"

"Darling," he said with the patience of a man discussing world events with a child, "we're talking about a grown man, a sane, rational adult—"

"No, we're not!" Julia insisted, shaking her head emphatically, ponytail swinging. "We're talking about Storm Dalton!"

She paced to the window that looked out on the waiting room and stood there staring, feeling like the only person in a horror film who knew the charming professor was in fact a pod creature intent on sucking everyone's brains out of their heads.

In a show of extreme frustration, Robert pulled his hands from his pants pockets and lifted them, palms up. "Well, I don't know what you want me to do. Should I call a judge and try to get a restraining order or something? What is it you want from me here, Julia?"

"I don't know! A reaction would be nice. Maybe a tiny show of concern."

"I shouldn't have to be concerned," he pointed out reasonably as he came to stand behind her. "You're not still in love with him."

It was a statement, not a question, holding not even a hint of uncertainty. Everything was cut and dried to Robert. It was one of the things that had attracted her to him—he was uncomplicated.

"Of course not," she said, trying her best to sound as calm and self-assured as he did.

"Then there's not a problem."

"Wanna bet?" Julia said, looking out across the waiting room to the glass double doors that opened onto the ambulance driveway.

Robert stared over her shoulder, jaw dropping, brows pulling together in astonishment. "What in the world . . . ?"

A float from the previous year's Aquatennial parade had rolled up in the parking lot on the far side of the emergency lane. Julia remembered it distinctly, because one of the people riding on the float had lost his balance and toppled off in front of her. She and a Shriners clown had administered first aid.

The float was covered in pale blue and silver sparkly, spangly stuff that shimmered like magic under the late afternoon sun. The call letters of a local country-music radio station were emblazoned across the side—KORN EARS TO FARM COUNTRY. The focal point of the float was an enormous cowboy boot fashioned from lumber, chicken wire, and an artful stuffing of brown paper napkins. The boot easily stood ten feet high. Seated on top, his own booted feet dangling over the side, was S.T., waving to the gathering crowd and grinning like a pirate.

"Storm Dalton?" Robert asked dazedly.

Julia shot him a plastic smile. "In the flesh, partner."

People poured out of the waiting room as if they

had been miraculously healed. They flocked around the base of the float like disciples, clapping and cheering, calling Storm's name. Julia ventured only as far as the door, loath to make an appearance and be singled out as the cause of this fiasco. But her conscience—and the fear that he would bring the parade indoors—prevailed and she pressed onward, Robert trailing after her like a dazed puppy. Poor man. She'd never seen him look quite so stunned.

A heart-wrenching country tune was crooning through speakers cleverly hidden inside fake hay bales, a song about a second chance for a fool in love. The driver of the float emerged from a hatch in the floor like the pilot of a submarine and started circulating through the crowd passing out carnations to the women and candy bars to the children and men. Julia stopped at the edge of the mob, not quite certain what she should do.

S.T. spotted her instantly. His blue eyes homed in on her like heat-seeking missiles and his grin widened. He dismounted from the boot, grabbing a rope that was apparently anchored to the top of his perch and lowering himself down the side like Robin Hood.

Scooping up an armload of pink carnations from the mountain of them on the float, S.T. hopped to the ground and strode toward Julia, his expression suddenly serious, his gaze intent on her face. Julia felt all eyes riveted on her. Murmurs ran through the crowd.

"He did this all for her."

"This is better than Richard Gere in *Pretty Woman*."

"Is this going to be one of those deodorant commercials?"

A television crew zoomed in on her with a portable camera.

S.T. didn't stop until he was toe-to-toe with her. The intensity on his face frightened her on a deeply instinctive level. This was the look of a male staking a claim. This was the look of a man who may seem easygoing and laid back on the surface, but underneath all that country charm was a bedrock of determination. When Storm Dalton wanted something, he went after it. And he wanted her.

He stopped in front of her, staring at her for a long second. The crowd held its collective breath. Someone snapped a photograph. Julia had the feeling she should have been making a run for it. Somehow she knew that when all was said and done and the dust had cleared she would look back on this moment and pinpoint it as the crucial second when she should have hoofed it but hadn't.

Suddenly S.T. swept his hat off, dropped down on one knee and said, "Julia, I've come to declare my intentions."

"I hope they include taking a gun and shooting yourself in the head," she growled through her teeth. "You'll save me *so* much trouble."

He went on as if he hadn't heard her. "I intend to win your heart, your love, your hand." He flashed a quick grin at the crowd and winked. "Well, shucks, I'll take all of her!"

Julia barely heard the cheers and laughter over her blood roaring too loudly in her ears. Her embarrassment threshold was not great to begin with. Between appearing in public in boxer shorts and this, it was pretty well maxed out.

Robert stepped around her, looking slightly embarrassed, and tapped S.T. on the shoulder. "Excuse me, but I really have to take exception to this."

S.T. rose to his feet, frowning. He recognized Dr. Bob instantly from the description Liz, his newly recruited spy, had given him—a life-size Ken doll, but not as animated—when he'd gone to the house again, only to find Julia had left for work. "Beat it, slick," he said under his breath, leaning aggressively toward the man who was his rival. "The lady and I have things to discuss."

"The lady is spoken for," Robert said evenly.

The hair on the back of S.T.'s neck bristled. His nostrils flared. "Oh, yeah? Well, I don't see a ring on her finger, and, if you get right down to it, she was mine first."

"But she's mine now."

"Not for long, Dr. Bob," S.T. said, warning giving his tone a sharp edge. "I intend to win her back."

"Is that a challenge, Storm?" a reporter called.

S.T. grinned like a wolf, his gaze still hard on the good doctor. "You'd better believe it, friend."

"How about it, sir?" the reporter asked, swinging a microphone in Robert's direction. "Do you accept the challenge?"

Robert shook his head, looking mildly amused. "I don't believe in that kind of thing."

S.T. stared at him, agog. He couldn't believe the man was staying so calm. If their places had been reversed S.T. was certain he would have flattened the guy's nose by now. He was here to take Julia away from this man. Didn't the guy care? Or was he just that sure of himself and his relationship with Julia?

"Excuse me," Julia said dryly. "Do you think I might have something to say about all this?"

All eyes turned toward her.

Julia looked from one man to the other—Robert, who looked like the captain of the debate team, calm and cool, designer perfect; and S.T., who looked like a cowboy ready for a fight, the wilder the better. Anger and embarrassment and frustration and confusion tangled inside her in one big knot. She could have taken Robert's arm and walked away, but she couldn't bring herself to do it. She was angry with him and not entirely sure why. That wasn't the problem with S.T.; she knew all the many reasons she was angry with him. What she couldn't explain was how she could look at him and see him for the heartbreaker he was and still feel . . . something. A part of her actually thought it was kind of sweet that he would go to all this trouble for her. What a hopelessly antiquated, unliberated thing to think. In that moment she fervently wished the male of the species would become obsolete and vanish from the face of the earth.

S.T. held up a hand before she could speak. "Time out. Back up here," he said, turning back to Robert, a look of consternation pulling his brows together. "Are you telling me you won't fight for her?"

Another wave of speculative murmurs rippled through the crowd.

"I don't believe in fighting," Robert said with a benevolent smile.

Anger stained S.T.'s high cheekbones and tightened his jaw. He took an aggressive step toward the doctor. "Are you telling me my Julia isn't worth fighting for?"

"She isn't *your* Julia."

"She damn well will be by the time I get through with you."

Julia rushed forward. "S.T., no!"

Her protest was cut short as he thrust two dozen pink carnations in her face. She grabbed the flowers in a reflex action and jerked them down, expecting to see blood. What she saw was S.T. and Robert nose to nose, with a television camera creeping in for a close-up.

"Two weeks, Dr. Bob," S.T. said, his voice low and thrumming with barely suppressed male fury. "Two weeks. All's fair. Winner gets the lady's heart."

He swung toward Julia, the trademark Storm Dalton grin breaking across his face as brilliant as the sun emerging from behind a thunderhead. Julia stared at him like a deer caught in headlights, knowing something was about to happen, but unable to make herself move to prevent it. S.T. grabbed her, dipped her like a tango dancer and kissed her hard, crushing the carnations between them. A roar went up from the crowd.

His face was beaming with excitement as he straightened and pulled back from her. His eyes were alight with devilish amusement, mouth curved in a roguish smile as he drawled, "I'm gonna win you back, baby. Let the games begin."

Four

"This is terrible!" Julia wailed, flinging the front section of the Sunday-morning *Star Tribune* on the kitchen table. She rose from her chair to pace the width of the small kitchen, her sneakers squeaking angrily on the tan linoleum floor.

Nibbling on a croissant, Liz craned her neck to take in the series of photos beneath the headline STORM SWEEPS BACK INTO TWIN CITIES. There was one of S.T. arriving at the hospital atop his giant boot, one of him kissing Julia's socks off, and one reaction shot of Julia after he'd released her. The photographs and accompanying article took up two-thirds of the page. Julia kept glancing at it as she stomped past, her temper spiking upward with each viewing.

Two-thirds of a page. Not even the most casual reader could possibly miss it. By noon most of the metro area was going to be aware of S.T.'s challenge to win her heart, and it was a sure bet who they would be rooting for. S.T. had always been enormously popular with football fans, even during his brief stint as a Viking, when he had been relegated to a backup position. He had always maintained a high profile with the public, lending his name and famous grin to advertising, lending his time to community charities. Word of him coming back to the Twin Cities would spread like wildfire. Word of his crusade to capture her heart would be the talk of the town.

"What are you complaining about?" Liz asked. "You got your picture in the paper! You were on the ten o'clock news last night! You're a celebrity. I would love it!"

"You're in fashion merchandising. Of course you'd love it. Look at me," Julia snapped. She leaned across the table and furiously tapped a photo with her fingertip so that her likeness jiggled animatedly. "I'm wearing a T-shirt with a brain on it! And my expression! I look like someone just got the drop on me with a cattle prod!"

Liz adjusted the rhinestone-studded reading glasses perched on her nose as she scrutinized the small print. "'Overwhelmed by Dalton's romantic gesture.' That's how they describe you here."

Julia gave an unladylike snort as she resumed pacing. Now that she'd had all night to stew about it, the faint glow of flattery had worn off completely, rubbed away by doubts and suspicions about S.T.'s motives. He was a man who thrived on challenge and limelight, and the previous night's folly had provided him with ample doses of both. Her opinion of the evening's events hadn't been improved by lack of sleep or a telephone that had rung off the hook until she'd nearly lost her voice saying "no comment" to the press. They had jumped on the story with all the enthusiasm of hyenas on a fallen gnu. She had finally unplugged every phone in the house.

"Romantic gesture, my fanny," she grumbled. "That was nothing but an ego-pumping, macho publicity stunt. If he thinks I'm going to fall for that kind of malarkey, he can just think again. I'm a liberated woman, for crying out loud. This isn't the Dark Ages. I won't be fought over by men and presented as the trophy to the winner."

Liz stared off wistfully, glasses slipping down her

nose. "Sounds like fun to me," she said on a dreamy sigh. "Two handsome warriors battling over me, their massive sweating chests heaving with exertion, the muscles in their arms standing out in taut bunches as they wield broadswords over their heads . . ."

Julia narrowed her eyes and shook a finger at her friend. "You know, you've been acting very strangely since you decided to get married. Listen to yourself. Pretty soon you'll be running around vacuuming the rug in little Donna Reed outfits with pearls and pumps."

"Forget it," Liz said with an indignant sniff. She pulled herself back to reality and her breakfast, tearing off another bite of croissant and popping it in her mouth. "Those shirtwaist dresses make my hips look fat. Besides, I'm sending out my signals exclusively to men who can afford housekeepers."

"Any luck yet?"

She made a face and shook her head. "I went to a bar mitzvah with my dentist last night. No chemistry. The most romantic thing he wanted to do was replace all my amalgam fillings for half price."

Julia gave a low whistle as she spread her feet and began a series of leg stretches. "Half price? Sounds like love to me."

Liz gave her a sly look and held up the newspaper beside her face, as if she were posing for a photograph. "It doesn't hold a candle to being 'Taken by Storm.'"

"He's not taking me anywhere," Julia insisted, straightening, her hands planted at the waistband of her navy-blue jogging shorts. "I'm perfectly happy right where I am. I've got a good job, a home, friends, Robert."

"Mr. Excitement," Liz droned, rolling her eyes.

"He's all the excitement I want. I don't need this kind of upheaval in my life," Julia said, pointing at the paper. "I just want a nice normal existence. I don't need a human tornado whirling into my life on a parade float."

Liz studied the photo of S.T. on the giant boot, puzzlement furrowing her brow. "Where did he get that thing?"

"Who knows?" Julia sighed as she moved back from the table, feeling physically drained even though she had yet to run a step. S.T.'s return was sapping her energy and leaving in its place a weird sense of fatalism. "The man has friends everywhere. I'd flee to Antarctica, but he probably has a fan club there. They'd hold me hostage until he could arrive by dogsled."

"What *are* you going to do?" Liz asked. "He seems awfully determined."

She was working a little too hard to appear non-chalant, like a gambler who wanted an inside line on the betting, but the effort didn't quite penetrate Julia's mood. Julia frowned as she extended one foot behind her and stretched her thigh muscle. "I'm going to avoid him like the plague for the next two weeks, and then take off as planned on my vacation. S.T. will eventually lose interest in his little game and go on to greener pastures." *I hope.*

Liz pushed herself away from the table, tightening her red silk kimono around her tiny frame as she went to the sink to deposit her coffee cup. Her eyes went round as she glanced out the window above the sink, but she recovered admirably before Julia could question it. She slid back into her chair and took up the paper again.

"Well, I think it's romantic," she said, her voice trilling like a lark's as she let loose a twitter of nervous laughter. "I don't see Dr. Bob making any grand gestures to prove his love to you."

"I don't need grand gestures," Julia said soberly. "I need stability. I'm going for my run."

A good, long, hard run, get the endorphins flowing, that was what she needed to clear her head. Running had always been her favorite therapy. Her subconscious could sort through her problems as her conscious mind focused on the scenery and the mechanics of planting one foot in front of the other. She loved the feeling of propelling her body along at a speed that released all her inner tensions, and God knew she had an abundance of inner tensions today.

She swung the front door open and her jaw dropped to her chest. Parked at the curb in front of her house was a fifteen-foot-tall fiberglass replica of a Hereford bull. It was the kind of thing supermarkets stood out by the street to advertise specials on steak, the kind of thing overbearing office acquaintances rented to stake out in the parking lot with witty messages like "Lordy, lordy, Edith's turning forty." The sign on the side of this one read: IT'S NO BULL, JULIA. I LOVE YOU. MARRY ME.

"My," Liz murmured weakly from behind her. "Isn't that sweet?"

The neighbors were wandering out across their lawns to examine the giant bovine wonder, looking Lilliputian beside it. Kids tore up and down the street on their bikes making cow noises and smacking kissing sounds. Already, two news crews had pulled in and were busy photographing the beefy billboard. Suddenly S.T.'s black pickup came roaring down the street, the German shepherd hanging his head out the passenger window, pink tongue fluttering like a banner in the wind. The truck pulled in behind the bull and S.T. hopped out to the applause and cheers of the crowd.

S.T. waded through the people, pausing to sign his name to five copies of the *Star Tribune* and one crumpled grocery list. He chatted amiably with the reporters, his mouth on autopilot, throwing out the tried-and-true Storm Dalton good-ol'-boy rhetoric as his gaze kept flicking to Julia. She looked stunned by the enormity of his gesture. He couldn't decide if that was good or bad. All he knew for certain was that he was damned relieved to see it was Liz standing behind her and not Dr. Bob.

He hadn't wanted to let her out of his sight after the scene in the hospital parking lot, but he hadn't had a choice. He couldn't dog her heels like a shadow day and night. He just had to trust what he had tasted in her kiss. She still had feelings for him. Not all of them were good, but she still had feelings. If he could draw them out and get her to face them, then maybe he could win her back. He was sure as hell going to give it his best shot.

The game plan he had come up with was brilliant. He would overwhelm her with grand gestures, a whole slew of them, actions that would leave Julia no doubt about his sincerity. He had spent half the night on the telephone, rousing old acquaintances from sleep to recruit them for his campaign, calling in old debts, planning his strategy. The rest of the night had been spent restlessly pacing his hotel room, wondering where Julia was and what she was thinking. At least now he had his answer to the first question.

"Last autograph, folks!" he called as he scribbled his name across the cuff of Mrs. Perkins's white terry-cloth robe. He shot them all a devilish smile. "I've got me a lady to win."

Mrs. Perkins patted his arm, her eyes twinkling like stars in the folds of her eighty-year-old face. "Go get her, Storm!"

He strode across the yard with his hands spread wide, his most incorrigible smile in place. The reporters trailed after him like a swarm of gnats, but S.T. ignored them. His attention was solely on Julia. "What can I say, Legs? The public is on my side. How do you like the bull?"

"It's appropriate, considering the source," Julia said dryly, arms crossed over the front of her faded gray University of Minnesota T-shirt.

S.T.'s smile faltered as he mounted the steps. "You don't like it?"

Julia had a sharp retort poised on the tip of her tongue, but she suddenly didn't have the heart to fire it. S.T. looked like a puppy that had just gotten scolded for chewing up shoes. He hadn't meant to embarrass her. He just had a tendency to let his enthusiasm carry him away. He'd always been like that.

"Well, it's very large," she offered. Not exactly a compliment, but it was the best she could do. She didn't want to encourage him or next time he would do something even more outrageous, like drop the cow out of the sky on a parachute.

"Biggest one I could find." He grinned and moved closer.

Julia stood her ground, even though all her nerve endings had gone on red alert, throbbing with awareness of him. He stopped a scant six inches from her, tilted his head a little to one side, and gave her a look brimming with sexual heat that was curiously, sweetly underscored by humor. The combination was an intimate invitation to share the joke, to laugh with him. It did strange things to her heartbeat.

"So, what do you say, baby?" he asked, lifting his brows. "Ready to give in?"

"You think you can win me over with a giant plastic cow?" Julia said dryly, valiantly fighting against the urge to smile. It was a losing battle.

S.T. leaned a little closer, bracing one hand on the door frame. "It's not the bull," he said, his voice hoarse and sexy. "It's the thought behind it."

"You should get a job with Hallmark," Julia quipped. "Sentiments like that belong on greeting cards."

"I've got better things to do with my time," he murmured, leaning a little closer, until his lips were almost brushing her ear. "Come have breakfast with me."

Shivers ran rampant over Julia's flesh, raising goose bumps in their wake. He might have just suggested they have hot, wild sex on the lawn, for the way her body responded. Her throat constricted, her breasts tingled, her knees wobbled, her toes curled in her shoes. It was the voice. He could read the *Congressional Report* in that tone of voice and make women swoon. Robert's voice never had that effect on her.

Another kind of shiver shot through Julia like a bullet. She stepped away, flashing a big phony smile. "Gee, this has been swell, but I've got to run."

Before S.T. could comment, she darted inside and headed for the back door. The word *coward* rang in her head as she bolted across the backyard and dashed for the alley, but it wasn't enough to make her turn around. Discretion was the better part of valor, after all. She charged down the alley, her legs eating up the distance. She needed to put as much space between herself and Storm Dalton as she could. She didn't like the things he could do to her with something as simple and innocent as an invitation to breakfast, rousing feelings in her she was better off without. He was like an addictive drug—bad for her, but tempting and seductive in an insidious way. He was exciting and sexy, but his cons far outweighed his pros. He was unreliable and unpredictable and she'd had enough of both qualities to last her a lifetime.

She was nearing the end of the block when a sound behind her penetrated her thoughts. She chanced a glance over her shoulder and saw the German shepherd bearing down on her, a big grin on his face as he loped along. But it wasn't the sight of the dog that made Julia's heart lurch; it was the sight of S.T. coming in hot pursuit on Andy Spader's fluorescent-green dirt bike. It was way too small for him. He looked ridiculous hunched over the frame, pedaling like crazy, his knees hitting the handlebars. But he was gaining on her.

Adrenaline pumping, Julia took a right at the end of the block and dashed across the street. The park on the other side was wooded and hilly; surely she would be able to lose him there. She hit a narrow dirt trail that cut through a stand of pine trees, the German shepherd right on her heels making little yipping sounds of excitement as he chased her. The mental image of wolves running an elk to the ground flashed through Julia's mind briefly, but she dismissed it. The dog might follow her, but he wasn't about to wrestle her to the ground and drag her back to his master. At least, she didn't think so.

Julia stole another quick glance over her shoulder. It was a major mistake. She knew it the instant she turned her head. As she looked back, she took a long stride, her right foot reaching out and finding . . . nothing.

She let out an involuntary cry as she tumbled down the hill in a tangle of arms, legs, and braid, bouncing over bumps and stones like a human ball, coming to rest at the bottom, flat on her back. She stared up at the sky for a second, her gaze focusing slowly on a cloud that appeared to be the exact shape of a cowboy boot. Then the dog pounced on her, panting and licking at her face.

"Ugh! Stop it!" she squealed, bringing her arms up to shield her face from a hundred pounds of over-enthusiastic canine.

"Bingo, off!" S.T. shouted from the top of the hill.

The dog flattened his ears and whined, slinking away with his tail down. He flopped down on the ground and put his head on his paws to pout.

Julia tilted her head back and watched as S.T. skidded sideways down the hill on the bike, holding the front tire at an expert angle to keep the bike from sliding out from under him. Where on earth had he learned to ride? She didn't realize she had voiced the question aloud until he answered her.

"Big Brothers in Kansas City," he said absently, abandoning the bike and rushing toward her. "My little brother was into racing the things."

He fell to his knees beside her, his expression taut with worry as he ran a trembling hand over her forehead and cheek. "Are you all right, baby? Are you hurt? Should I call an ambulance?"

"I'm okay," Julia said on a groan as she started to sit up.

S.T. held her down with a hand on her shoulder. "Be still," he ordered, beginning an inspection of her limbs. "You might have broken something."

"I didn't break anything," Julia said irritably, batting his hand away. "I'm a nurse, remember? I know these things."

"You could be in shock."

She was in shock all right, but it had nothing to do with the fall she'd taken. She'd been in shock since she'd opened the door Saturday and found him standing on the other side. And if she let him examine her further she would probably go into some kind of hormone-induced seizure.

"I'm fine, S.T.," she mumbled. "Nothing wounded but my pride."

He allowed her to sit up, but remained poised to grab her if she showed any inclination toward fainting. Julia did her best to ignore his look of concern as she took stock of herself. It wouldn't do for her to be overly touched by his anxiety. She glanced down the length of her arms and legs, taking in dirt and minor scrapes but no major damage. Tomorrow she would be spotted with bruises, but that was nothing considering she could have broken her neck. It was a good twenty feet to the top of the hill and the descent was steep.

"You scared ten years off my life," S.T. said, a tremor of leftover fear rattling in his voice. "You're sure you're all right, honey? You could have a concussion." He stared hard into her eyes, assessing the state of her pupils, then raised the last three fingers of his left hand in front of her face. "How many fingers am I holding up?"

Julia made a face and started to give a sassy answer, but the words stopped in her throat as her gaze caught on his pinky. Her heart gave an enormous thump in her chest. He still had it. He still wore it. The cheap dime-store friendship ring she'd given him that summer back in Montana, with a chip of glass that no one in their right mind would mistake for a diamond. She'd pretended it meant they were engaged, even though she'd been only sixteen and had known he was going off to college in the fall.

"You still have it," she murmured. A wave of emotion threatened to break over her. This sentimentality was dangerous stuff. She told herself she couldn't let it rule her head, but she couldn't keep it from affecting her heart. As the memories besieged her, she reached out and caught his hand, drawing it close so she could have a better look.

It wasn't a pretty hand. His fingers had sustained much damage during his football career. Some bent in directions never intended by nature, and the skin of his palm was rough and callused like a cowboy's. The ring looked like it was worth exactly what she'd paid for it—$1.98. The glass chip winked at her, flashing under the summer sun.

"It's a wonder it doesn't turn your finger green," she said dryly, trying to minimize the emotional impact with wry humor.

S.T. looked her in the eye, his expression suddenly almost unbearably tender. "It does," he said softly. "I wear it anyway."

The tears were there before Julia had a chance to blink them back. They brimmed in her eyes and blurred her vision. She let go of his hand and turned away from him as she struggled to her feet.

"Damn, this ground is hard," she grumbled, busying herself with dusting the dirt off her seat and legs.

S.T. rose slowly, watching her. He wanted to pull her back to him and remind her of the day she'd given him the ring. He could have told her that he'd kept it all these years because it was a way of having her close. He could have told her of the long nights he'd lain in his bed staring at the ceiling, holding that ring in his hand and thinking of her. But he let the moment pass; those memories would probably scare her with their intensity.

"Here, let me help you with that," he offered, resurrecting his devilish smile as he reached for her behind.

Julia twisted out of reach, giving him a look. "Not a chance, Dalton."

"Gee, honey, you used to like to have my hands on your—"

"Ancient history," she declared sternly.

"You used to like to have my hands all over you," he pointed out in a warm, dark voice. Slowly he backed her toward a big maple tree, his blue eyes dancing with mischief.

"Past tense," Julia said. She hit the tree and pressed against it, wishing she could dematerialize and pass right through it.

"Yeah, I'm past being tense, all right," S.T. murmured, bracing his hands on either side of her head.

He leaned closer and closer, until she could feel the heat of his body radiating through his clothes and hers. His gaze held hers with an intensity that was almost hypnotic. "I'm just about going crazy wanting you, baby."

Julia's heart fluttered in her throat like a trapped bird. "S.T., no—"

Her protest was once again swallowed up by his kiss. It was warm and sweet and soft. Julia couldn't help but melt beneath it; it was too compelling, too familiar, too good. He took his time, as if they could have stood there all day and done nothing but explore the myriad nuances of this one kiss. He changed angles subtly, altered the pressure imperceptibly, moved his tongue against hers in lazy, sensuous strokes.

Caught up in the heady mix of memory and new desire, it was impossible for Julia not to be mesmerized. It was impossible for her to not respond. Their bodies had been in tune with each other since that summer day by the lake when she had given him her virginity and he had given her the kind of love she had yearned for all her life.

He leaned into her now, his solid chest against her breasts, his hips finding hers. Their heights were almost a perfect match, bringing them into contact in all the crucial places. His belt buckle pressed against her belly, and his manhood nudged her feminine mound, seeking satisfaction. His thighs brushed the insides of hers as he sought to get closer.

Julia groaned low in her throat. Her arms wound around his ribs, her hands splayed over the taut, rippling muscles of his back. Of their own volition her hips tilted to accommodate him, to invite him, and he arched against her, reminding her vividly of the size and shape of him, making her ache deep within.

"That's it baby," he whispered against her lips. "Want me. Want me."

Want him. She'd done nothing but want him since she was sixteen. The trouble was, while she may have always wanted him, he hadn't always been there. He'd taken his fill of her love and left her every time, left her wanting something he'd never been willing to give. He claimed he was ready to give it now, but old habits were hard to break and old hurts hard to heal.

S.T. felt the change in Julia's mood. It was like a sudden frost killing the warmth that had been ready to explode between them. His heart sank. He'd pushed too hard, tried to take too much too soon. He had tried to coach himself to be cautious, but he never had been much for taking direction. Even if he had been more obedient, it was just nigh unto impossible for him to get within two feet of Julia and not want her. With a weary sigh he ended the contact before she could push him away.

He stood back, head down, hands on his hips, one leg cocked in an unsuccessful attempt to alleviate the discomfort of his arousal straining against the front of his jeans. He looked askance at Julia. She had stepped away from the tree and was staring off toward a small pond in the distance where couples and young families were walking idly and throwing popcorn to the wild ducks. The expression on her face was one of worry; not anger, but uncertainty tinged with guilt. Her brows drew together; her lush mouth tightened and turned down at the corners.

"Why are you doing this, S.T.?" she asked without looking at him.

"Because I love you," he said simply.

She shook her head, causing her long fraying braid to wiggle against her back. "You can't just come and go in and out of my life as you want and call it love. That's not love, that's convenience. I'm all through being Julia McCarver, Disposable Woman."

Anger surged suddenly inside S.T., the heat of it suffusing his face with color. He grabbed Julia by one arm and turned her to face him. "It was never like that," he said emphatically. "I always loved you, I just always found a reason to get out before I could blow it. I was scared, Julia."

"And you're not scared now?"

"Scared spitless," he whispered. "But what I'm most afraid of is losing you for good."

Julia looked into his eyes, a part of her wanting to read truth there, a part of her wanting to see a lie. She didn't want him back in her life. The risk was too great. But still, there was that part of her that had always needed him to need her. They had been soul mates. That was hard to throw away.

"What are you going to do after the two weeks are up?" she asked, moving out of his grasp. Maybe if she made it clear enough he wasn't going to win this stupid challenge, he would give up now and save them both a lot of grief.

He gave her a look of unswerving determination. "Take you back to Montana with me and live happily ever after."

Julia sniffed. "Forget that. I'm staying right here. I have a good job, a good life, a nice guy—"

"Do you love him?" S.T. took hold of her arms again, turning her so he could see her face.

"What kind of a question is that?" she said on a forced laugh. "I'm going to marry him."

He shook his head, his bright-blue gaze boring into her like spotlights that would show any hint of untruth. "That's not what I asked. I asked, do you love him. Do you love him the way you used to love me?"

She frowned prettily. "Robert is a very good man. We have lots of common interests—"

"Do you love him?" he repeated, enunciating each word carefully.

For the life of her, Julia couldn't look him in the eye and answer. She tried, but the words couldn't seem to find their way out of her mouth. A big ball of fear swelled up inside her and stuck at the back of her throat. Of course she loved Robert. Of course she did. Then why couldn't she say it?

A hint of a smile canted S.T.'s mouth as relief washed through him. He would have died if she'd said she was in love with Dr. Bob.

He brushed a stray curl from Julia's cheek with the pad of his thumb and murmured, "That's all I needed to know, sweetheart."

He let her go and stepped back. His good humor returned with a giddy rush, lighting his eyes and spreading a big Cheshire-cat grin across his face. "You might as well pack your bags, baby," he teased. "You belong to me!" He sang out the last line in a booming baritone that drew stares from people yards away.

Julia scowled at him. "Eat dirt and die, Dalton. I don't belong to anyone and I won't be a prize in your stupid macho contest. If you have such a burning desire to win something, go buy a lottery ticket. And now I have to go," she muttered, glancing at her watch. "I have a luncheon meeting."

"What a coincidence," S.T. said with a big saccharine smile. "So do I."

Julia eyed him warily, rubbing absently at her upper arms where he'd held her. Her heart began a long slow slide toward her stomach. "Not the Wish Foundation."

He answered with a shrug. "What can I say? I'm a member of the national board, you know. Isn't it lucky I'm back in town just in time for the big fund-raising events?"

"Yeah," Julia mumbled weakly. "Lucky. Lucky me."

Five

Julia told herself she had no right to be angry. S.T. was the one who had gotten her involved with the Wish Foundation in the first place; it only stood to reason he would still be involved. Whatever else he may have been, he was unfailingly loyal to his community obligations. It was one of the things that had made him so popular with fans.

While other sports celebrities were busy throwing their money around and making headlines with their brushes with the law, Storm Dalton was busy visiting hospitals and working with underprivileged youth. He had become a national spokesperson for the Wish Foundation, a charity that helped bring joy into the lives of seriously ill children by trying to grant wishes such as trips to Disneyworld and meetings with celebrities. Julia still got choked up over the television commercial he'd done on behalf of the foundation, asking people to give to the United Way.

So she had no business being angry because the local board of directors was fawning all over him. She had no business being angry because the fund-raising activities were suddenly centering around him or because the press had followed him here. The additional coverage the foundation would get because of him would be a blessing. But she *was* angry.

It was a primal thing. This was her turf now, and S.T. was invading it. He was invading every aspect of her life. And the fact that he had a legitimate reason to be here didn't change the fact that he also had an ulterior motive—her.

Julia sat at the long luncheon table twisted up like a pretzel, her arms crossed tightly in front of her, her legs crossed under the table, one foot tapping angrily against a table leg. Before her sat an untouched glob of chicken salad on a curly doily of lettuce, a beacon to salmonella germs from far and wide. Beside her sat Vera Creighton, man-hungry socialite extraordinaire.

It was widely known that Vera considered charity groups a great untapped source for men, and prowled from one to the next like a lioness in heat. Vera hadn't taken her eyes off S.T. from the second they had been seated for the luncheon. She was a woman of perfect height and lithe build, decked out in a flame-red designer suit. She had classic features, a suspicious lack of wrinkles for a woman of forty-four, and the kind of hairstyle that must require the wearer to sleep upright—a confection of ash-blond ringlets that were shaped and trimmed into an alluring "I'm rich as sin, but a gypsy at heart" look. Julia imagined the hairstylist trimming it with shears, like a gardener at a topiary bush.

"God, isn't he just yummy?" Vera purred. "I've always said these charity boards are the places to snag a good one. I mean, if you go looking in a bar, what are you going to wind up with? A drunk. If you go to health clubs, they're either gay or worried you're going to be prettier than they are. Come to these luncheons and what do you find? Generous rich men with social consciences. Let me at 'em!"

Julia couldn't think of a single thing to say. S.T. was standing at the head table giving an impromptu pep talk to the troops. He did look yummy. He'd changed from his usual jeans and work shirt into stylish pleated tan trousers and a pale-blue polo shirt that brought out his tan and made his eyes look more brilliant than sapphires. The belt and silver buckle he wore were still cowboy attire, as were his boots, but instead of looking incongruous they only added to his image of masculinity.

"Oh!" Vera chirped in Julia's ear, her eyes rounding with imitation surprise. "I forgot. He's after you, isn't he, darling? Of course, I saw that in the paper. What a dreadful photo of you. That was really too bad."

She offered her condolences as if someone had died. Julia ground her teeth. Luck had suddenly turned against her with a vengeance. First S.T.'s invasion of her life, now lunch with Vera. She wouldn't have wished this woman on her worst enemy.

"Well, he's out of bounds," Vera pouted, tossing her head like a distressed runway model. "Bad luck."

A nasty smile suddenly tugged at the corners of Julia's lips as she glanced up at S.T. "Oh, gee, Vera, don't let me stand in your way. I've got one fella. Two would be hogging."

Vera's eyes lit up. She came to attention in her chair like a hunting dog scenting a quail. "Really? You mean it?"

Julia chuckled to herself as she pictured S.T. fending off Vera the Voracious. "Sure. Have at him."

" . . . and Storm has generously offered to donate his time to the annual Wish Foundation picnic," Harvey Benton, president of the group, announced from the podium at the head table. All present applauded enthusiastically. "We've decided to give him a committee of his own to help coordinate his activities with the children." Harvey's long face lit up with a coy little smile. "Naturally, he has requested Julia Mc-Carver to be his assistant."

Julia narrowed her eyes at S.T. as the rest of the group made sounds of amused approval. "And Vera can help us out too," she offered cheerfully, baring her teeth in a parody of a smile that was instantly captured on film.

Vera cooed her delight.

A muscle twitched in S.T.'s cheek, but his smile didn't waver.

As the meeting adjourned there was the usual confusion of people moving, conversations mushrooming in clusters. Vera made a beeline for S.T. behind the podium and attached herself to his side like a barnacle, beaming up at him with a blatant "take me, I'm yours" look that brought a flush of embarrassment to S.T.'s cheeks.

"I just love you in those deodorant commercials," she purred, false lashes flapping like hummingbird wings. "You look fantastic in a ripped undershirt."

"Thanks." S.T. managed a smile. He tried to edge sideways a step. Vera remained wound around his left arm like a vine.

"'When things get exciting—Stay Cool,'" she whispered, leaning into him, one hand trailing down his chest. "Shall we put your motto to the test, studmuffin?"

S.T. jumped back in the nick of time, his eyes going moon-wide with shock as Vera just missed her target. His gazed homed in on Julia. She waved her fingers at him as she backed away from the table.

He broke out of Vera's grasp in a move he'd perfected on the football field to avoid being sacked—ducking and rolling right, making his way toward Julia as she made her way toward the door. Vera, however, had an eye for angles that would have done an NFL linebacker proud. She cut him off at the corner of the table, a feral gleam in her eyes.

"Now, don't be shy, darling!" she cooed, bearing down on him. "Teamwork is what a committee is all about!" She latched onto his arm again and whirled him around to march him back toward the front of the room, slanting him a come-hither look. "Come along, cowboy. Be a good boy now and later we'll play bronco."

Julia paused to get one last look at S.T. as Vera led him away. She tried to muster a giggle at his predicament, but the sight of him with another woman on his arm left her with a vaguely sick feeling. She tried telling herself it was indigestion. It certainly wasn't jealousy. She couldn't possibly be jealous when she'd sicced the woman on him in the first place.

Feeling unsettled, she turned to make her escape, but Harvey Benton caught her by the elbow.

"Not so fast, young lady," he said with a fatherly chuckle. "We want to get some pictures of you and your beau for the paper."

"Harvey, he's not my beau," Julia corrected him patiently.

Harvey was the CEO of a major toy manufacturer based in Plymouth. Power and prestige came with the job, but Julia suspected he enjoyed the idea of being a Santa Claus figure more than anything else. At sixty-plus he looked on everyone younger than he as a favored grandchild. He was benevolent and sweet and was obviously getting a big kick out of playing Cupid's helper.

"There's no need for you to be shy about it, Julia. We've all seen the papers."

"Great."

"Now we'll get a nice picture of you two lovebirds," he said, adding under his breath, "if we can peel Vera away. . . ."

S.T. took Julia's arm as Harvey herded her into place. "Thanks for rounding up my gal for me, Harvey."

"My pleasure, son!" Harvey said with a chuckle. He let go of Julia, stepped to S.T.'s other arm, and took hold of Vera. "Come along, Miss Creighton. We can discuss the plans for the picnic."

Vera snarled at him like a cornered Doberman. "Take a hike, Harvey. I've got plans of my own."

They faced each other, bumping and shoving as Harvey pried her fingers off S.T.'s arm, both of them flashing big toothy smiles in case the press caught them.

"Now, Vera—ouch! Goodness, those heels are sharp!"

As soon as his arm was free, S.T. edged himself and Julia away from the scuffle, smiling for the cameras the entire time. Julia sent him a lethal look that was camouflaged by a thin smile.

"Aw shucks, Mr. Dalton," she drawled through her teeth. "Maybe you oughta just put your brand on me, so's I wouldn't get my little self lost."

S.T.'s eyes flashed with humor and heat. A predatory smile flicked up the corners of his mouth as another picture was taken. "That sounds like a grand idea," he murmured. "Maybe we can discuss it in depth later, say after dinner in the privacy of my hotel room?"

"Sure." Julia smiled so hard she thought her lips would crack. Another flash went off. "When pigs fly."

To their left, Vera wriggled free of Harvey's grasp as he tried to lead her aside. She bolted back to S.T. and grabbed hold of his arm, clinging to him like a limpet. "And a picture of the three of us!" she demanded with a sparkling look at the cameras. "We'll be working so closely together," she said to S.T., snuggling against his side. "Except Julia, of course. She's so busy with her job and her *boyfriend*."

Julia grabbed the cue, determined to get out. "Speaking of busy, I really must go." She wrenched free of S.T.'s grasp, waved to the room in general, and headed for the door at a fast walk. She glanced over her shoulder to see if any of the press people were following her, but they were sticking to S.T. like burrs on a dog, crowding in on him to ask questions about his involvement with the Wish Foundation.

She hurried out of the meeting room and down the plush hallway to the lobby of the hotel, her heart pounding with every step. Maybe, just maybe, she was going to make a clean getaway. A uniformed doorman opened the door for her and she stepped outside, her gaze homing in on her Firebird in the parking lot.

Bingo was sitting in the driver's seat.

The dog's ears perked as he watched her approach. He panted happily as she walked up to the car, but the minute she reached for the door handle he started barking. The windows had been rolled down and the barks boomed like cannon fire, the car acting as a natural amplifier. Julia jerked her hand back from the door. Bingo looked up at her, eyes shining, tongue dripping doggie drool all over her upholstery. Once more he looked happy to see her, but when she reached for the handle again he set up a racket that would have scared ten years off a mailman's life and that turned the heads of people at the hotel entrance.

"Bingo, this is *my* car," Julia said. Embarrassment and anger brought a burst of warmth to her face. Out of the corner of her eye she saw a man in uniform coming toward her. She reached for the door again. Bingo let loose another cannonade of deafening sound.

"Is there a problem here, ma'am?" the security guard asked as he came up beside her. He could have been Bill Cosby's humorless brother, big and grim with one hand resting on the butt of his giant flashlight, ready to subdue her should she try anything untoward.

Julia managed a wan smile. "This is *my* car, but this *isn't* my dog."

The man gave her a skeptical look as he pulled a pen out of his pocket and prepared to take notes. "You're saying someone put a guard dog in your car without your permission?"

"Yes."

The guard stared down at her for a long moment, apparently waiting for her to crack and confess to her life as a master car thief. When Julia only shrugged he said, "I think we'd better go inside, ma'am. The police can clear this up."

Julia closed her eyes and counted to ten. She was going to get S. T. Dalton for this, and then she was going to find a new hiding spot for her spare car key. When she opened her eyes he was standing beside her, grinning amiably at the security guard.

"It's all right, sir. That's my dog," he said sheepishly. "I guess he prefers the lady's company, but then, I can't say that I blame him."

The guard's face lit up with recognition. "Hey, you're Storm Dalton!" he exclaimed, pointing at S.T. with his pen.

"In the flesh, partner."

"Oh, man!"

S.T. shook the man's hand, autographed a security violation ticket for him, and sent him on his way with his face wreathed in smiles. Julia stood leaning against the hood of her car with her arms crossed, waiting, glaring at S.T.'s back. The man was a menace. He could charm nuns right out of their habits if he put his mind to it.

"Booby-trapping my car! What a rotten trick, Dalton!" she growled at him when he turned back toward her.

S.T. made a face as he let Bingo out of the car. "No worse than you siccing Vera Creighton on me." He shuddered. "I think I'm going to need rabies shots."

"All's fair," Julia quipped, batting her lashes at him. "You made up the rules, cowboy."

"That's right, and I intend to play by them."

The words and the look that accompanied them seemed subtly ominous. He stood across from her, leaning against his pickup, the breeze ruffling his hair. He had his hands in his pockets and his stance seemed casual, but there was an underlying tension in the set of his jaw and his broad shoulders. Julia glanced askance at him, wary. "What's that mean?"

"It means that you can throw all the hurdles you want in my path, but they won't make a bit of difference."

He took a step toward her, reached out and caught a strand of her hair, rubbing it between his fingers in a gesture that dated back to the beginning of their history. The determination in his gaze warmed and softened to something that caught at Julia's heart. He was the same old S.T. in many respects, but at moments like this she sensed a difference in him. Quiet was the word that came to mind. Where there had always been a sense of restlessness, there was now a sense of quiet about him that came from deep within. She wondered at its source, at its meaning, but she wouldn't allow herself to ask.

He let go of her hair and brought his hand up, forefinger crooked under her chin, tilting her face up slightly so she looked him directly in the eye. "Stop running away from me long enough for us to have a real conversation," he said softly. "Have dinner with me tonight. We'll talk."

For just a second she was tempted. She could feel the strong, steady lure of his magnetism and the tug of old memories. Then from the corner of her eye Julia saw the front doors of the hotel swing back and spew forth a sea of newspaper and television people who headed straight for them, shoes thundering on the pavement as they moved en masse. Her mouth twisted in a wry smile as she opened her car door and settled down into the bucket seat. "Just me and twenty or thirty of your closest media pals? No thanks. I've already got a date."

S.T. stood back, hands on his hips, and watched her drive away. He tossed off a grin and a cute remark to the press as they gathered around him, but he didn't hear any of their questions. The woman he loved had just run away from him again, and she was headed straight for the arms of another man. He was going to have to do something about that.

• • •

In the history of dates, this one was not going to rank anywhere near the top, Julia thought as she shifted in her theater seat. Robert had arrived to pick her up precisely on time, making no mention of S.T. or the newspaper. He hadn't brought her flowers or candy or any other token of romance. Julia told herself she hadn't expected any of those things, that, as a liberated woman, she didn't need or want them; she couldn't be bought with a few chocolates or overpriced posies. Still, she had caught herself feeling disappointed. Robert was making no effort to woo her at all. He seemed to be pretending the challenge had never been made.

She looked up at the movie screen and sighed. The film was in Swedish, the grim, tragic story of an immigrant farm woman's lifelong struggle against nature and sexist oppression in nineteenth-century Minnesota. Heartwarming stuff. It seemed to have been going on for about nine hours. Julia took a peek at her watch. Sixty-seven minutes had passed since the opening scene of a woman in the throes of labor amid a hundred seasick people in the filthy hold of an immigrant ship. She glanced at Robert. He seemed enthralled, eyes flicking left to right as he read the subtitles.

Julia shifted again, trying to stretch surreptitiously. She let her attention wander away from the screen, where the valiant, starving heroine was stumbling along behind a plow. Checking out the rest of the moviegoers held more potential for entertainment. It was a small, trendy theater in Uptown that brought in movies no one ever heard of outside of Cannes. The place was more than half full of people sipping bottled water and munching gourmet popcorn, eyes glued to the screen.

She seemed to be the only person not even pretending to be engrossed in the exploits of the intrepid

Helga. The guy behind her was actually panting along with the heroine. Julia bit her lip to keep from groaning in disgust as little puffs of fetid hot breath stirred against her neck, and leaned hard to the right side of her seat. Maybe the guy was some new upscale breed of pervert, getting off on foreign films instead of porn.

Taking care to appear casual, she turned her head to steal a glance and caught a tongue on her cheek. A big, slurpy dog tongue. Bingo sat in the seat behind Robert, leaning forward to sniff them. Julia jerked around farther, coming face-to-face with S.T. He was wearing a false beard and a big smile.

"Oh my God," Julia groaned. "How did you get that dog in here?"

S.T. flipped down a pair of square black sunglasses from the top of his head as he leaned forward in his seat. "I told the ticket girl he was a seeing-eye dog. Man, this movie is a real yawn. Does he drag you to this kind of thing all the time?"

Robert turned around and shushed him. "We're trying to concentrate on the film."

S.T. pushed his sunglasses up and rolled his eyes. "I'd rather watch grass grow."

The house lights came up for a brief intermission, giving everyone a respite from Helga's suffering. Julia stood and stretched, her gaze hard on Robert. "I'm really not enjoying this, Robert. Could we just go home?"

He stood slowly and brushed the wrinkles out of his trousers, frowning. "We can't let him ruin our evening, Julia."

"I'd have to go some lengths to top this awful movie," S.T. said dryly, leaning a hip against the back of Julia's seat. "Good move, Dr. Bob. You scored a lot of points with this one. I take all my dates to movies where they not only get to watch pain and suffering, they get to read every word of it as well."

"The women you date can read." Robert lifted a tawny brow. "Now there's a surprise."

Julia scowled at him. "Hey, what's that supposed to mean? *I* dated him!"

"But you don't anymore."

"That's about to change, Dr. Bob," S.T. said with a smile. "You're losing here, big time."

Robert gave him a look of mild amusement. "I'm not competing with you, Dalton."

S.T. laughed. "You got that right, partner."

"Julia is an adult. She can make her own decisions—" Robert's placid argument was cut short by his beeper. He gave Julia an apologetic look. "That's going to be the hospital. I'll have to go. I'm sorry."

Julia waved him off. "I'll be okay. Go save a life."

"A plastic surgeon?" S.T. asked skeptically as he watched Dr. Bob hurry out of the theater. "What's he going to do—an emergency nose job?"

"He does a lot of work with burn victims," Julia explained. "Infection after a skin graft can be deadly."

S.T. did his best to stifle a sigh. How the hell was he supposed to compete with a man who saved lives? He'd been just a football player—not important in the grand scheme of life, no matter how big a deal the media made out of it. He brooded as he watched his rival disappear through the swinging doors to the lobby.

They hadn't kissed. The thought struck him like a tiny hammer that made his reflexes jump. Dr. Bob hadn't kissed Julia good-bye. She hadn't leaned up to give him so much as a peck on the cheek. For an allegedly engaged couple there was a decided lack of passion between them.

He thought back to the kisses he had shared with Julia in the past day and a half. They may have had their problems, but a lack of passion was not among them. So what was it that had her running away from him and into the arms of a man who had all the warmth of a mannequin? He glanced at Julia, catching her watching him with that guarded, wary look, and the answer came to him as plainly as if she had spoken it aloud. Safety. She couldn't be hurt by a man she didn't love.

"So, what do you do when he has to run off like that?" he asked.

"Call a cab."

"Not tonight, you don't," he said, seizing the opportunity. "Come on, let's blow this place and go get a pizza."

Julia looked scandalized. "I can't go out with you! I'm out with Robert."

"Who seems to be conspicuously absent. Come on," he said with a coaxing smile. "You've got a night off from work. Why waste it on a cab ride to Bloomington when you could spend it with me?"

"Because I'll be safer in a cab."

"You're safe with me!" he said, looking as if he couldn't believe she wouldn't trust him. The expression somehow very easily altered into one of his wicked teasing smiles. "That is, unless you don't think you can keep your hands to yourself."

Julia slanted him a look as the house lights began to dim.

"Come on," he said, nodding toward the aisle. "Before we get stuck watching the rest of this turkey."

"I'm not going with you," she said as she followed him to the lobby. "I'm just going."

S.T. flipped down his sunglasses and jammed a baseball cap on his head. He took a tighter hold on Bingo's leash and let the dog lead him through the lobby. Julia followed them onto the street. The sun had gone down, but the sky was still light in the west, ablaze with shades of orange and pink. The dusky light combined with neon window signs gave the renovated buildings of Uptown a soft, nostalgic glow. The night was warm and pleasant. There were people out on the sidewalks, some power walking, others browsing in shop windows. None of them stopped S.T. for his autograph. The press was nowhere in sight.

Julia walked beside him, her hands in the pockets of her baggy khaki walking shorts. She wore an old white T-shirt with a faded "Life Run" logo on it. Her hair had escaped the comb Liz had swept it back with on one side and it hung loose, the evening breeze teasing the ends. She had felt underdressed with Robert. With S.T. she felt as comfortable as the worn deck shoes on her feet. It was difficult to worry about appearances with a man who had seen her in her first real bra.

Their relationship had never really had much of anything to do with looks, anyway. What had united them had been way beyond animal attraction and the usual rites of courtship. It had been rooted in a sense of kinship between two kids no one else had understood, a sense of kinship that came from understanding each other on a deeply elemental level. As she walked beside him now she realized that if she let down her guard, let go of her wariness, she would still feel that sense of kinship with him. It didn't seem a smart thing to do, all things considered.

They left Bingo to guard S.T.'s pickup and ducked into a new pizza place in Calhoun Square. S.T. ordered without consulting her, already knowing her preference—Italian sausage, extra mushrooms, light on the cheese. As the waitress walked away he scratched at his phony beard.

"Great disguise, huh?"

"You look like Steven Spielberg," Julia said with a wry chuckle. "We're lucky we weren't set upon by movie groupies. Why are you in disguise?"

"Undercover work," he said, sitting back, chewing on a bread stick. "I wanted to see what I was up against. What does he have planned for your next date, a trip to the dentist?"

"He doesn't usually do this badly."

S.T. tilted his head to one side and narrowed his eyes. "I got to tell you, Legs, I don't see you with this guy. He's all wrong for you."

"And you were all right?"

"I will be this time."

Julia looked away and shook her head as the waitress brought their sodas.

S.T. took a sip of his drink and decided to let the subject drop. He couldn't argue her into wanting him again.

"So," he said resolutely. "For the picnic I thought I'd call some of my cronies from the Vikings and get them in on it. They're good ol' boys, and they'll be glad to show up. And I've got a few contacts in the sporting goods lines. I figure I can get a bunch of footballs and whatnot to give away, and— What?" Julia was looking at him as if she had been suddenly struck with amnesia and had no idea who he was. "You don't like those ideas?"

"No, I mean, those are great ideas. It's just that— well—I didn't know how serious you were about helping, beyond showing up with your press pals in tow."

S.T. sat back in the booth with a harsh, humorless bark of laughter. "I'll be the first to say I deserve a few kicks from you, but I don't deserve that. The foundation picnic may be providing me with an opportunity to spend some time with you, but my first obligation is to the kids."

Julia could have crawled into a hole. Unfortunately there wasn't one around, so she was forced to sit there and suffer S.T.'s critical scrutiny. She'd hurt his feelings and she felt like a slug. It was one thing for her to be angry with him concerning their personal relationship, but she had questioned his sense of duty, and that was uncalled for. S.T. was unswervingly loyal to his charity work, determined to give kids a better childhood than the one he had endured.

"I'm sorry," she said, frightened by how badly she

wanted his forgiveness. She couldn't bear the idea of him being angry with her, any more than she could bear the idea of hurting him. "I know you'll do a great job. I guess I'm just feeling a little crowded, that's all."

"Crowded?" He feigned surprise, splaying a hand against his chest. "By me?"

Julia caught the twinkle in his eye and couldn't resist the smile that tugged at her mouth. That was S.T.: quick to anger, quick to forgive, quick to tease.

The waitress brought their pizza and they ate in companionable silence, an unspoken truce in effect. When they were finished S.T. paid the bill and they walked out onto the street, ambling in the direction of his pickup, neither of them in a particular hurry.

"So, how do I shake Vera?" he asked.

It was Julia's turn to feign surprise. She gave him a look of wide-eyed innocence, batting her lashes. "Why do you want to shake her? I thought you made a lovely couple."

S.T. scowled. "You wouldn't believe the things she whispered in my ear before Harvey dragged her away. Let's just say money isn't the only thing she wants to see raised. She left messages at my hotel that made the desk clerk blush."

Julia chucked. "You could tell her you're gay."

"Very funny."

They had reached the pickup. Julia leaned back against the passenger door, hands in her pockets, dark eyes sparkling under the light from the street lamp. S.T. soaked in her appearance like a sponge, memorizing the way she looked—relaxed, happy, pretty in a way that had more to do with her spirit than her face. A jolt of love hit him like a solid boot to the chest.

"I could tell her we're engaged," he murmured, leaning close.

"We're not."

He bent his head and brushed his lips against her ear. "We could be."

"S.T. . . ." she said on a groan.

He pulled back just enough to take in her expression. It was troubled again, uncertain, wary. "I guess I'd better get you home."

Julia looked up at him, the disappointment in his eyes touching her in a place she didn't want to be touched. "I think that would be best," she whispered.

The drive out to Bloomington was a quiet one. Traffic was light. S.T. seemed lost in thought. He turned the radio to a country station that apparently saved all its sad and poignant songs for the evening. One heart-wrenching tune after another drifted out of the speakers as he sat back, right hand on the steering wheel, left arm resting on the open window. Bingo had been positioned between them, but he wanted the window seat and wasn't shy about making his preference known. He sprawled across Julia's lap, pinning her in place like a hundred-pound seat belt, and stuck his head out the window to let his ears flap in the breeze.

Julia rubbed the dog's broad, muscular back absently as she studied his master's face in the dim light of the dashboard instruments. She could read his emotions in the set of his jaw, the line of his brow. She could feel them in the air. The loneliness that had linked them in the beginning was there. Now that he had abandoned the bravado and the bad-boy grin it showed through in big, raw patches. Julia caught herself wanting to reach out to him. She didn't want him to feel alone, she didn't want him to feel hurt, but she didn't want him in her life, either. He was at another crossroads, and there was just too great a chance that she would get left at the corner again when the light changed and he moved on.

He pulled up in front of her house and cut the truck's engine, turning the key back so the radio could continue sighing out soulful emotion. When he turned to her he had resurrected his smile. It flashed like a wedge of moon in the darkness of his false beard.

"See?" he said with a shrug. "Here you are, in one piece, virtue intact."

Julia gave him a little smile. "You were a perfect gentleman."

"Yeah, well, don't tell anybody. I've got an image to maintain, you know."

"Your secret is safe with me."

"So," he said, easing toward her, right hand inching along the back of the seat. "I got to have Dr. Bob's date, do I get his good-night kiss too?"

Julia sniffed. "Not a chance, Dalton."

That was all she needed, another of Storm Dalton's patented toe-curling kisses. She already felt as if she were teetering on the precipice of a very high cliff. She couldn't escape the feeling that if she touched him now the ground beneath her feet would crumble and fall away.

He leaned a little closer, showing every sign that he was going to help himself and steal the kiss if she wouldn't give it to him. That was S.T. He played by the rules until they turned against him. He was an outlaw at heart.

Julia pressed back against the door, fingers fumbling for the handle. She was still weighed down by Bingo, who had settled against her, his massive head resting on his forepaws on the open window.

"Aw, come on, Julia," S.T. coaxed, his voice as warm and soft as flannel. "Just one little kiss?"

As his mouth brushed over hers several things happened simultaneously. Julia lifted the door handle. A cat ran past on the sidewalk. Bingo lunged forward, intent on the cat, hurling himself out of the truck and giving Julia a mighty shove as he went. Julia gave a little *whoop!* of surprise as she fell backward, automatically grabbing S.T. and pulling him with her. They landed in a tangle on the grassy boulevard, Julia on her back with S.T. sprawled on top of her. He raised his head and smiled dreamily.

"That was some little kiss, sweetheart," he drawled. "I think the earth moved."

"I'll move you!" Julia gave him a shove that didn't budge him. "Get off me, you—you—kiss bandit!"

He obeyed reluctantly, pushing himself to his feet with a wince and a groan. He held out a hand to Julia. She looked at it as if she expected to see a joy buzzer tucked against his palm, then accepted it anyway and let him pull her up. Bingo came slinking back, head hanging, demoralized at having lost the cat amid Mrs. Perkins's shrubbery. Julia shot the dog a glare, then turned to S.T., who was gingerly rotating his right shoulder, face pinched as he worked the kinks out.

"I think I'm wounded," he complained.

"Well, it's no more than you deserve," Julia groused. "Stealing kisses like a teenager." She could still feel the imprint of his body on hers. The contact had awakened nerve endings better left asleep.

"All's fair," S.T. reminded her.

Julia ground her teeth and made a wild sound of frustration in her throat that elicited a worried whine from Bingo. "Your stupid challenge!" she exploded, shaking her fists like maracas. "That's all you're thinking about—winning. Well, you're not going to win me, cowboy. Give up and go away."

"Give up?" S.T. said, arching a brow. His manner had shifted swiftly from teasing to determined. He planted his hands at his waist and shook his head. "Give up and let you marry some man you don't love, just because he's safe? Oh no, sweetheart. I can't let you do it. I'm not about to give you up. In fact, I've only just begun to fight."

Six

On Monday all of the radio stations in the Twin Cities began "Storm Watches," keeping close tabs on S.T. and his efforts to win Julia's heart. One station devoted a large portion of its morning drive-time show to a call-in program where listeners could give suggestions as to how S.T. should go about the job. The most outrageous suggestions won prizes.

On Tuesday the television campaign began. In addition to a series of "Julia, be mine" commercials, S.T. gave interviews to all the local stations concerning the upcoming picnic and gala fund-raising ball for the Wish Foundation, assuring the interviewers that both he and Julia would be present at the events. Advance tickets to the ball, at 150 dollars a pop, sold out by midafternoon.

On Wednesday the billboards went up.

Julia found herself an instant celebrity, recognized while standing in line at the drugstore with a box of tampons in her hand, set upon by members of the Storm Dalton fan club while filling up her car. She was even hounded at the hospital by reporters who claimed to have everything from gangrene to typhus, all of them angling for an exclusive.

It was unnerving, to say the least. As she had

predicted, everyone in town was rooting for S.T. and they made no bones about it, jumping right into the spirit of the competition. She even received a few letters from people eloquently urging her to marry him.

She was alternately angered and charmed by S.T.'s efforts. The small things charmed her and tugged at her heart, the gifts that arrived mysteriously on her doorstep—a nosegay of hand-picked violets with a clumsy-looking bow tied around the stems, a plastic heart charm from a gum-ball machine, a pair of dangling earrings in Bingo's likeness. The small things reminded her of the tough young cowboy with the hidden sensitive side she had first fallen in love with. The grand gestures made her question his motives. They reminded her of the star athlete who loved to win, the man who loved the spotlight. The grand gestures were overwhelming in their grandeur. Every time she looked up along the freeway and saw a nine-foot-tall version of S.T.'s wicked grin beside a cartoon balloon saying JULIA, BE MINE she was reminded that this was a contest and Storm Dalton meant to win it.

By Friday of the first week she was exhausted. Julia dragged herself through the front door, abandoned her shoes in the foyer, and stumbled down into the living room, where she fell across the sofa with a dramatic groan.

Liz was sitting in her favorite chair enjoying a glass of white wine, stockinged feet propped on the coffee table. She had yet to change clothes from her workday and looked like something out of a fashion magazine in a neon-green Spandex miniskirt and a psychedelic tunic. A necklace and earrings that were seemingly fashioned from Tinkertoys completed the ensemble. She gave Julia a look of sympathy tinged with amusement. "What did he do today?"

Julia sighed. "Caused a riot at the supermarket. I don't know how he does it. The man seems to know every move I'm going to make. I stopped on my way home from work to get the stuff you had on that list and there's S.T. on the sidewalk, dressed in a fish costume and carrying a big sign that read 'Julia, I'm just a poor sucker in love. Marry me.'"

Liz laughed, then defended herself against the black look it won her. "Come on, don't you think that's kind of sweet? I mean, how many men would be willing to do that?"

None that Julia knew of. She certainly didn't see Robert making a fool of himself over her. He had done nothing out of the ordinary over the course of the "contest." He had insisted he wasn't competing with S.T. He had shown no signs of distress over the campaign S.T. was waging. He went on as usual, calm and unflappable, while Julia's nerves were getting tied in knots.

All she had to do was hang on for one more week, she reminded herself. One week and she could escape. She would climb on a plane and head to California for two glorious weeks of socially acceptable laziness. She clung to the idea of getting away from the pressure, going off on her own to a quiet beach. She closed her eyes and pictured it as she had a hundred times in the past two weeks. Blue water, soft white sand, lying in the sun dozing, listening to the waves sigh against the shore, opening her eyes and seeing S.T.—

She jolted upright on the couch, heart pounding. "I've got to change. Robert's picking me up at seven."

Liz rolled her eyes. "Where's he taking you this time? A yawning festival? A staring contest? The man should have his own television program— *Lifestyles of the Dull and Boring.*"

"He's taking me to dinner at Madrid," Julia said smugly, pushing herself to her feet. "And frankly, after what S.T. has put me through this past week, dull and boring sounds just great to me."

Twisting her Tinkertoy necklace around her finger,

Liz fixed her with The Look of Great Wisdom. "Maybe now you say that, but how does it sound for the rest of your life?"

Safe. The answer came instantly, but Julia didn't speak it aloud. Instead, she turned and headed for the solace of a hot shower. As the water poured over her she couldn't get out of her head S.T.'s parting words the night he'd dropped her off. He claimed she had chosen Robert because he was safe. What was wrong with that? People chose mates for worse reasons. Robert was even tempered, stable. Life with him would be predictable. Life with S.T. would be an emotional roller-coaster ride—wild highs and belly-scraping lows, never knowing what might be around the next corner, never knowing when the ride was going to end.

Safe sounded pretty darn good to her.

She dressed with her usual careless disregard, throwing on a simple black tank dress that hugged her figure, panty hose, black flats. When she appeared in the living room Liz shook her head, casting her eyes heavenward, and marched her back into the bedroom to accessorize her, adding dramatic gold earrings, a cuff of thin wire bracelets on one wrist, and a long black chiffon scarf that wrapped once around her neck with the ends trailing down her back. She pronounced the results "stunning." Julia just looked in the mirror and shrugged. She had applied her makeup with her usual light hand and left her hair in its natural wild state, too tired to attempt to subdue it. She thought she looked passable and only hoped her hair wouldn't find its way onto her dinner plate. Robert disliked social gaffes.

He picked her up at seven on the dot, looking his usual immaculate self in dark pleated trousers, white shirt, conservative tie. They drove downtown to the restaurant in the quiet comfort of his BMW, Julia's stomach rolling over every time they passed one of the pink billboards that announced S.T.'s intentions to the world. When she told Robert of S.T.'s latest stunt at the supermarket he only smiled and chuckled.

Julia's stomach churned harder as she watched him. "Isn't this getting to you at all, Robert?" she asked in a small voice.

He glanced over at her with a smile. "The man is making a fool of himself, Julia."

Because he loves me. The instinct to defend S.T. rose up inside her like a mother tiger's need to defend her cub. She said nothing, but slumped down in her seat and stared at the armrest as if it might hold the answers to life's great mysteries.

The Madrid had established itself as one of the favorite dinner spots for young professionals in the Twin Cities area. The decor was Mediterranean—rough white stucco walls, Moorish arches, lots of dark carved wood and black wrought iron. The Spanish theme didn't carry through to the menu, however, which boasted salads, pastas, chicken breasts prepared in numerous imaginative ways, vegetables presented in artistic arrangements.

Julia ordered something called North Woods Breast of Chicken, "a marinated breast of free-range chicken portrayed on spinach fettucine with a complement of pine nuts and artichoke hearts." It came complete with a garnish of tiny pinecones and evergreen needles. She found herself staring at it and wondering what the folks back in Montana would have to say about "free-range" chickens. The mental image of cowboys riding out to round up the flock made her put her fork down and cover her mouth to stifle her laughter.

Robert looked up and from his meal and raised an eyebrow. Julia let him in on the joke, but he didn't get it. He just smiled politely and nodded, retreating to doctor mode in the face of confusion.

S.T.'s voice drifted through Julia's head like a wisp

of smoke. *I got to tell you, Legs, I don't see you with this guy. He's all wrong for you. . . .*

He wasn't all wrong, she insisted. He was just different. They complemented each other.

A strolling musician had begun to wind his way around the tables, nimble fingers plucking out melodies on a twelve-string guitar. He was on the far side of the room with his back to them, but the music still drifted to their table. Julia found herself listening instead of eating. It wasn't the kind of driving, dramatic Spanish music one might have expected in a place called Madrid but simple, sweet songs with an American folk feel to them. They made her think of Montana and the mountains, the way the meadow grass rippled in the wind, the way the lake looked under a blue sky. They took her back to a time when love had seemed simple and S.T. had played his beat-up six-string for her on summer nights.

The guitarist was making his way toward their table. He was dressed the same as the waiters—black trousers, white shirt, black jacket. Julia never caught a glimpse of his face. He always seemed to be turned the other way. But her nervous system went on alert, like a radar sensing the approach of an enemy attack. She began watching the expressions of the other restaurant patrons as they looked up at him, their eyes lighting with recognition, mouths leaping into smiles of surprise.

Julia's skin prickled as if she had just stepped into a highly charged electrical field. The music ended to a round of enthusiastic applause from the crowd. S.T. turned and smiled down at her.

"And now, if you all won't mind putting up with my rusty voice for a minute, I'd like to do a special song for the lady of my heart," he said, his blue eyes homing in on Julia's face with an intensity that made her breath catch.

His fingers moved surely over the strings and he began to sing, his husky voice rich and warm. The song was a familiar one to Julia. The lyrics had been stored away in her memory, never to be forgotten. S.T. had written the song for her and had taken her to their special place by the lake to sing it for her the first time. She remembered the day as if it had just happened, remembered exactly the way she'd felt as she sat there and listened to the ex–bad boy of Muleshoe sing his heart out for her.

It was a love song, honest and simple and sweet. And in the magical way of songs it reached inside Julia and touched her in a place nothing else could have. She sat there and listened, mesmerized, emotions floating to the surface like bubbles that had been trapped in the bottom of a pond. When he finished, the silence in the room was absolute.

Perhaps it was Robert who started the applause, but Julia wasn't sure. She couldn't think at all. She couldn't bring herself to do anything. She just sat there like a zombie, staring up at S.T., and he stood there looking down at her, his expression one of naked longing.

At that moment, with time hanging in the air around them, Julia realized she still loved him. It was the thing she had been most afraid of—not that he could make her fall in love with him again, but that she had never stopped loving him in the first place. In spite of everything he'd done to hurt her, she had never stopped loving him. She would probably always love him. It didn't matter where he went, what he did, how many times he left her. There would always be some integral part of her that would always belong to him.

"Now, that ought to win her for me, hadn't it, folks?" he drawled, drawing good-natured laughter and cheers from the other diners.

Julia stood up without a word and walked out.

S.T. watched her go, his smile faltering, his heart sinking. He'd had her. For a second there she had been within his grasp and he'd felt all the raw fear and need and love he'd felt at eighteen, when she'd been the only person in the world who really understood him. For just a moment time and place had ceased to exist, and it had been just the two of them, soul mates, like old times. And now she was walking away.

He watched her head for the exit with long strides that stretched the fabric of her dress against her backside and made the ends of her scarf float out behind her like streamers. Somewhere in the dim reaches of his consciousness he heard the scrape of a chair against the tile floor, then Dr. Bob brushed past him on his way out. An elderly lady sitting at the table on his left reached out and slugged him on the leg with her fist.

"Go after her, dummy! I've got money on you!"

S.T. bolted for the door, running smack into a busboy with a cart of dirty dishes. China crashed, flatware flew, the cart spun around, and the busboy too. S.T. plunged on, narrowly missing a waiter and almost knocking the hostess flat. By the time he made it to the parking lot Christianson's BMW was already pulling out onto the street.

"Damn!" He turned and gave the right front tire of his truck a vicious kick. The action swung his guitar against the fender, and the instrument sent up a discordant protest at the abuse. S.T. silenced it, closing his left hand over the neck in a grip that threatened to crack the wood.

Bingo hung his head out the open truck window and whined. Heaving a defeated sigh, S.T. leaned back against the door, reaching up blindly to stroke the dog's head.

"Well, Bingo," he said, eyes still on the street where the BMW and Julia had disappeared. "Looks like I blew it again."

"What did you want me to do, Julia?" Robert asked, exasperated, lifting his hands in what was for him a gesture of supreme agitation. "Stand up and punch him in the mouth? That would have made me look quite the hero, wouldn't it? Beating up a man who'd just sung his heart out for you."

Julia paced back and forth beside the car, arms banded tightly against herself. She felt on the ragged edge of hysteria, tears pressing up behind her eyes, panic swelling in her chest like a balloon. She couldn't say what she wanted from Robert, but whatever it was she wasn't getting it. He leaned against the hood of his car and crossed his arms over his chest, the furrow between his brows the only indication that he was at all concerned.

"You could have said something," she snapped. "You didn't have to just sit there like it didn't concern you."

"What could I have said? More to the point, when could I have said it? You bolted and ran the minute he was finished."

"I don't know!" she shouted, flinging her arms up. Her hair swung into her eyes and she tossed it back with an angry shake of her head. "All I know is I've been enduring this stupid contest for days and you haven't done a damn thing!"

Robert gave her a long, grave look usually reserved for delivering bad news to the terminally ill. "I shouldn't have to compete with him, Julia," he said softly. "You either love me or you don't. Maybe you should just think about that for a while."

A brittle silence descended between them. He stared at her for a long moment, his expression inscrutable, then he turned to go. He didn't kiss her. He didn't touch her. He climbed into his BMW, backed out of her driveway, and headed toward Minnetonka.

Julia stood on the concrete drive, staring after his taillights as the peaceful night settled around her. It was warm. The stars looked like silver glitter scattered across the sky. Somewhere down the street kids were playing basketball, the ball *thunk-thunking* against the ground as they dribbled. It seemed surreal to her, calm and normalcy all around while a storm raged through her life.

Her nice, safe future was crumbling around her like a ruin in an earthquake. She could feel it all coming apart at the seams, the structure twisting apart under the stress. The security she had longed for all her life was slipping out of reach.

"Damn you, S. T. Dalton," she murmured, raking her hair back from her face with both hands.

A light was on in the living room and the Gipsy Kings were wailing out of the stereo speakers. Liz sat on the floor in a yoga position, eyes squeezed tight as she let out a long howl.

"What are you doing?" Julia yelled, wincing at the assault on her ears.

Liz ended her yowl abruptly and glanced up. "I'm sending out new signals."

"To whom? The natives of Borneo?" She stuck a finger in her ear and wriggled it back and forth. "They're probably racing for the nearest airport."

Liz ignored the sarcasm, her sharp gaze reaching easily past Julia's barriers. "Tough night?"

Julia rolled her eyes as she toed her flats off. Liz's own vibrant energy seemed subdued, like a gas jet that had been abruptly turned to low. Evidently they had both struck out in the game of love. "What's your story? I thought you had a date with a hot prospect."

The face Liz made was reminiscent of someone tasting castor oil for the first time. "I think I've been sending out defective signals. First it was my dentist; then Max the UPS man, who was in transition from breaking up with his significant other; then Raymond, who turned out to be into all this weird kind of Zen sex thing. Now Wilmar."

"What was wrong with him?"

"Aside from his name, he was obsessed with his own mortality. How can you think of commitment with a man who wants to talk cemetery plots over cappuccino?" She gave a shudder of distaste. "Maybe I was wrong about this being the right time for me to get married. Maybe this is a sign I should become a nun or something. What do you think?"

"Don't ask me. Personally, I've had it up to here with romance." Julia sliced a hand across her throat. "I'm going to bed. Tomorrow is going to be the longest day of my life."

She doubted she was going to sleep any better than she'd slept the past week, but at least she would be in the privacy of her own room as she went insane. She changed into a white silk sleep shirt and went through her nightly ablutions, her mind crowded with the image of S.T. as he'd looked down at her, the last notes of his song lingering in the air like the faint scent of wild flowers. She had almost believed he meant it when he said he wanted to be with her forever.

She still loved him. The realization brought no joy. Everyone she'd ever loved had left her—her mother, her father, S.T. They had taken her love and vanished, leaving her alone and lonely, longing for something she could hang on to, someone she could trust.

She trusted Robert, trusted him to remain constant, trusted him not to hurt her. He couldn't hurt her because she didn't love him, she realized, facing a truth S.T. had seen from the beginning. Robert was a good man. She respected him and liked him, but she didn't love him. He was right—he shouldn't have had to compete with S.T.; if she loved him he would have a firm hold on her heart.

So where did that leave her? she wondered as she stared up at the ceiling above her bed. Alone again. She didn't love the man she could trust and she didn't trust the man she loved.

The music came so softly she almost didn't notice it. The melody drifted in through the open window, floating on the breeze, sweet, clear notes, like bird song coming from far away. Julia pushed back the covers and went to the window. S.T. sat in a lawn chair on the deck, one booted foot propped on a tub of geraniums. His face was partially illuminated by the yellow glow of Mrs. Perkins's back-porch bug light. He had shed his head-waiter outfit in favor of old jeans and a white T-shirt that molded his broad shoulders. His hair was mussed, as if he'd run his fingers through it over and over, strands of black tumbling across his forehead. He strummed the last chord of the song and looked up at her, his expression pensive.

"I wasn't sure you'd be here," he said, pushing himself to his feet. In fact, he had been terrified she would be gone. Visions of Dr. Bob soothing her with kisses had been tormenting him for the past hour. It would have been the perfect chance for the good doctor to press his advantage. He wondered whose decision it had been for them to go their separate ways.

"And if I hadn't been here, would you have given up?"

He stared at her through the screen, determination overriding the worry and the weariness. "No."

Julia leaned against the window frame and sighed. "Oh, S.T., what am I going to do with you?"

He gave her a weak, lopsided version of his famous grin. "For starters, you can let me in."

"Let you in to my bedroom?" Julia laughed.

The smile faded. The longing welled up in him like a tide, just to be near her, just to hear her voice, just to have her there, his kindred spirit, his friend. He was so afraid of losing her, he was almost choking on it. "Please," he whispered.

Julia was silent for a long moment. She studied his face in the dim light. There was no hint of the man who had paraded in front of the supermarket in a fish costume, no sign of the brash rogue whose grinning face loomed over the metro-area freeways. This was just S.T., and he needed her to say yes.

She opened the screen and S.T. crawled through, guitar in one hand, crumpled brown-paper bag in the other. He leaned the guitar carefully against the wall and presented the bag to Julia.

She eyed it warily, taking hold of its very top. "If there's a box of condoms in here, you're a dead man."

S.T. slouched against the wall, hands in his pockets, a boyish light in his eyes as he watched her. "It's a present. Open it."

Julia flicked on the small bedside lamp, raised the bag, and studied it. "Well, I don't think it's a billboard, and if it's a cow, it's a small one."

"Zip the lip and just open the bag, McCarver."

She flicked him a look but obeyed, setting the sack on the nightstand. Her expression as she peered into the bag was priceless—a completely spontaneous reaction that combined surprise and pleasure and remembrance. She lifted out the one-pound bag of M&M's as carefully as if it were a priceless piece of crystal and clutched it to her chest.

"You remembered."

"Of course I remembered," he murmured. "I remember the time I snuck them to you in your room when you were grounded because we stayed out too late at the county fair."

"I was so depressed because I was going to miss the fireworks and I knew all the kids would give me a hard time afterward, because I was the only person on earth who had to stay home." She looked down at the bag in her hands as if it were a magical fragment of her past. "And you skipped the show and brought me M&M's to cheer me up."

"It was my fault." He pushed himself away from the wall. "Just like tonight was my fault. I never meant to upset you, Julia." His smoky voice hoarsened even more and he glanced away from her, jaw working, lashes blinking. "I just keep wanting to show you how much I care, and I just keep messin' it up. I don't know what else to do."

Julia's hands tightened on the bag of candy. "I know you care, S.T."

"I love you."

"I know."

She turned away from him and walked to the window. Mrs. Perkins had turned off her porch light. The lawn was cast in shades of darkness. She could make out the shapes of the lawn chairs, the picnic table, Bingo stretched out on top of it, waiting patiently for his master. She looked up at the stars. When she was sixteen she had looked up at those same stars and wished on the brightest one that S. T. Dalton would love her.

He slid his arms around her from behind and snuggled close, rubbing his cheek against the back of her head. "I don't want to fight with you tonight, baby. I'm tired of fighting. I grew up fighting my old man. Spent a long time fighting myself. Spent the last couple of years fighting to hang on to my career. I'll fight for you till the day I die, but tonight I just want to *be*. I just want to hold you."

Julia could feel his loneliness, his pain, reaching out to her as they always had, echoing her own feelings. He was her soul mate, the other half of her heart. If she turned him away she would be alone, and alone was the last thing she wanted to feel tonight. There were too many hard questions waiting for her in the quiet of the night, too much emptiness stretching out ahead of her.

S. T. knew her answer the minute she turned in his arms and looked up at him. She didn't have to speak. He read her easily, intuitively. He told himself if he'd been a nobler man he would have asked her if she was sure, if this was what she really wanted. But he wasn't feeling noble, he was feeling needy. He wouldn't question her reasons, wouldn't risk having her turn away. He'd been too long without her and their future was too uncertain.

His mouth descended on Julia's, settling against her with a hunger and urgency she matched instantly. He brought trembling hands up to frame her face, touching her with infinite care, his fingertips brushing the baby-soft tendrils of hair at her temples. He cupped her face like a chalice and drank deeply from her, savoring the taste of her, letting her flavor fog everything else from his mind.

Julia did the same, letting go of every thought except one—that this was the only man in the world she had ever truly loved. She needed his touch, needed him with an intensity that set her on fire. She would take what she could tonight and not worry about tomorrow. She welcomed the thrust of his tongue against hers, the feel of his lean, hard body, the crushing force of his arms as they banded around her. She slid her arms up around his neck and dropped the bag of M&M's as the hardened points of her nipples brushed the solid wall of his chest.

Her every nerve ending seemed on fire, hypersensitive to S.T.'s touch. Her body was so in tune with his that it responded of its own accord, without any conscious thought on her part. She pressed into him as he bent her backward, her hips arching into his as he trailed kisses down the column of her throat.

He fumbled with the buttons in the front of her nightshirt, opening three before giving up. The white silk slipped away from her, like quicksilver on her skin, falling open to reveal breasts that were high and firm with dusky nipples pouting for attention. Julia gasped as he brushed his knuckles gently across one turgid peak, sending a firestorm of desire roaring through her, a fire that only burned hotter when he lowered his head and took her nipple into his mouth. It swirled through her leaving her dizzy and weak and hungry beyond anything she'd ever known.

Nearly frantic to feel his skin against hers, she

pushed him back and tore his T-shirt from his jeans, shoving it up to reveal a taut belly corrugated with muscle, a perfectly carved chest. As he pulled the shirt off over his head and flung it aside, she bent her head and kissed the crooked scar above his right nipple. Then her lips trailed downward, fastening on the hard button of flesh, winning her a groan as she rubbed her tongue against it.

S.T. caught her by the shoulders and pulled her up against him, his hands sweeping down her arms, pushing off her nightshirt. It puddled at her feet like a drift of melting snow and was forgotten as he hauled her up against him and took her mouth once more. They both gasped as they came together, flesh to flesh, breast to chest, belly to belly.

His belt buckle was cold and bit into her stomach but Julia ignored it, too caught up in other sensations to care. His chest was warm and hard, the muscles of his shoulders like stone beneath her hands. His arousal nudged her, straining against the front of his jeans, and she pressed into it, her own body just as hungry and eager as his.

"Oh, baby, I need you," he whispered against her mouth. "I've missed you so."

As if to illustrate the point, he pulled her left hand down and closed her fingers around him through his jeans. Julia stroked him, adrenaline and desire pumping through her veins in equal portions as she measured his length and hardness with her fingertips. Her mind rushed ahead, reminding her of how it had always been between them, hot, unrestrained, unselfconscious. The memories heightened the anticipation until she was trembling.

He kissed her again as he backed her toward the bed. His tongue plunged into her mouth over and over until they were both gasping for air. The backs of Julia's knees hit the edge of the bed and she fell back across the mattress, pulling S.T. down with her. He sprawled over her, his head on her chest, mouth seeking and finding her breast as his hands swept down her sides to her hips, fingertips catching in the waistband of her panties and rolling them down. He kissed his way down her belly, over her hip, down the long length of one thigh as he slipped the last of her clothing off, then sat up to pull his boots off.

Julia watched intently as he stood and reached for his belt buckle. His gaze caught on hers and he turned slowly toward her as he unhooked the big silver oval and slid the tooled leather belt free. Neither spoke, but the communication between them was intense, thickening the air with electricity. Julia drew her eyes down from his face, over his chest and stomach to where his hands rested at the waist of his jeans. He popped the button free from its mooring and she caught a little gasp in her throat as if the action had startled her. He eased the zipper down, dropped the jeans, and stepped out of them, kicking them aside. When he reached for the waistband of his briefs, Julia stopped him.

"Let me," she said, sitting up.

She slid her hands over his lean hips, brushing over the soft white cotton of the briefs. Catching her fingers in the elastic band, she drew them slowly down, freeing him to her gaze, her touch. Leaning forward, she pressed a soft kiss to the point of his hip and another at the crease of his thigh.

S.T. groaned deep in his chest. He tangled his fingers in her hair and held her to him for a moment, closing his eyes in ecstasy as she gave him the most intimate of kisses. But even as pleasure sang through him, he caught her arms and pulled her up.

"Not this time, baby," he murmured, planting swift kisses along her jaw. "I want you too much."

They sank back down on the bed together, legs tangling. S.T. slid a hand between them, his fingers probing the tangle of damp curls between Julia's thighs. She opened herself to him, arching her hips in invitation, gasping as he tested her readiness by easing two fingers deep within her.

"That's it, baby," he whispered against her ear. "Hot and wet. Ready for me."

"Please," Julia gasped.

"You want me, Julia?"

"Yes."

"Say it," he commanded as fierce possessiveness roared to life inside him. "Look at me and say it. Say you want *me*."

Julia looked up at him, feeling helpless. She wanted him. She had always wanted him. "I want you, S.T. Love me."

"Oh, I do, baby," he murmured, his gaze locked hard on hers. "I do."

He watched her face as he entered her. She took him into her body, tightening around him, searing him with liquid heat. She was his, had always been his. He reclaimed his rights in a ritual as old as time.

They moved together in a perfectly orchestrated ballet. Needs reached out to needs, desires intertwined until their feelings seemed as one. And when the end came it was in an overwhelming explosion that shook them both to their very hearts.

Julia felt herself floating, adrift on a sea of sensation. It was lulling and intoxicating. A part of her wanted to go on drifting, but another part of her was frightened by the feeling, afraid she would drift so far out she wouldn't be able to get back to the safety of solid ground. If she let herself become entranced by the seductiveness of the sensation she might never escape. She couldn't afford to let herself become too entangled in S.T.'s sensual web again. They had needed each other tonight, but she wasn't betting her heart on any promises of tomorrow.

S.T. leaned over her, tenderly brushing her hair back from her face. His expression was intense, concerned, a worry line creasing between his brows as he looked down at her.

"Don't regret this, baby," he whispered.

"I don't."

"The hell you say." He tapped a forefinger against her temple. "I can see you circling the wagons in there already. Rounding up the troops to defend against me."

"I have to protect myself, S.T.," she said honestly. "I don't regret making love with you, but I'm not dropping my guard to take another sucker punch."

Julia could see the hurt in his eyes as he moved away from her, and she could have kicked herself. He was trying so hard to convince her of his sincerity, he probably didn't even realize that most of his efforts were frightening her off rather than getting her to believe in him. She rolled onto her side, her body automatically snuggling against his as he lay on his back staring at the ceiling.

"I'm sorry," she whispered, nestling her head against the pillow of his shoulder.

"Aw, don't be," he drawled, kissing the top of her head. "I know I screwed up. So what happened with you and Dr. Bob? I can't believe he's not the one lying here holding you instead of me."

Julia flinched inwardly. "I'd rather not talk about Robert, if you don't mind."

"Mind?" He gave a snort of disbelief. "Hell, maybe my luck's turning around after all. I was starting to think I'd left it all back in Kansas City."

"Why did you leave?" Julia asked abruptly. She was eager to turn the topic away from her relationship with Robert, a relationship she was no longer certain she knew the definition of, but she was also curious about what had gone on in S.T.'s life in the past year. When he had been with the Vikings he had seemed nowhere near ready to give up his career, regardless of criticism that his arm was going and his knees were shot.

"Leave K.C.?" He gave a little shrug. "It's not home. You weren't there."

His answer was simple and honest. Julia's heart did a little flip-flop, which she did her best to ignore. "I mean football. Why did you quit now? You had a great year."

He was silent for a long moment. When he began to talk his voice was soft and smoky, tainted with a touch of wryness and a touch of sadness. "Last season was a gift from the big guy upstairs. One last hurrah for old Storm. I'd been hanging on by a thread the last two or three years, you know that. When I was with the Vikes I was so afraid of getting cut loose I could hardly see straight. That was part of the reason I left you the way I did.

"I felt like a failure, like I was sliding down a long, steep grade to nowhere. I didn't want to drag you down it with me. I'd spent so long being Storm Dalton, I didn't know what would be left when that was gone. I'd gone from being Bud Dalton's no-account kid to being a golden boy, but all the gold was wearing off and I was afraid that when it was gone there wouldn't be nothing left but that no-account kid, grown up and gone worthless just like his daddy."

"You were never like him," Julia protested, remembering the mean-tempered, violent drunk who had raised S.T. They had lived on the ranch north of her aunt and uncle's place. On clear nights the sound of Bud Dalton's angry voice had sometimes carried all the way down the valley. She could still remember Aunt Clarisse's tight look of disapproval and the clucking of her tongue as random notes of drunken rage had reached their ears on the front porch. It still cut at her heart to think of the hellish parody of childhood S.T. had been forced to endure.

"My old man used to tell me day and night I'd never amount to spit," he said. "I just figured the football thing was kind of a fluke, a big joke on all those people who suddenly couldn't get enough of me, that one day the punch line would hit and everybody would see I was just exactly what they'd thought in the beginning—good for nothing."

Julia raised herself up on one elbow and looked down at him in shock. "You never told me you felt that way!" she said, hurt that he had held something back from her at a time when they had shared everything.

His smile was sad as he combed a strand of red hair behind her ear. "How could I tell you, baby? You were the one person who really believed in me, in S.T., not some gridiron god. How could I tell you I thought I was nothing? What would you have believed in then?"

Julia said nothing. She sank back down beside him and settled an arm across his chest, fighting to keep herself from squeezing him with all her might. She thought back to that first summer, how sweet he had been, wanting to give her something, wanting to live up to all her girlish notions of who he was behind the bad-boy grin. And he had felt compelled to keep up the facade all this time. "What happened in Kansas City?"

"I learned some things about myself. I found out there was a lot more to S. T. Dalton than the sum of his football talents. I spent a lot of long, lonely nights thinking about what was really important in my life. When I got the chance to play again I proved I could fight for something and win it. My knees were about gone and the arm had lost its thunder. I had to get the job done on guts and brains, and I did it. So I had my last stand in the spotlight and I went out a winner. Now it's time to move on."

He reversed their positions, rolling Julia onto her back and caressing her body with his as he settled on top of her, taking his weight on his elbows. She looked up at him, trying to assess the changes in him. There was that same familiar twinkle of mischief in his eyes, but there was a certain weariness too. He still possessed that same vibrancy, that same force of personalty that had made him a celebrity, but there was also a sense of peace about him, a calm that hadn't been there before.

"All I want to do now is ranch all day and make love with you all night," he said softly. "And make babies," he added with a heart-stealing smile. "Would you have my babies, Julia?"

Julia felt something like the flutter of wings in her chest. How many times over the years had she pictured a dark-haired baby boy nursing at her breast? How many times had she longed for that with all her heart? But babies needed daddies and S.T. had never stuck around long enough for her to believe the fantasy could become a reality.

Did he really see her as something more than a challenge to be won? Was there a chance she could be something more than a comfort stop at this crossroads in his life? Did she dare take the chance of finding out?

S.T. watched the war between logic and emotion raging in Julia's dark eyes as she looked up at him. A part of her wanted to answer yes to his question. That was good enough for him tonight.

"You know, I can think of better things for us to do tonight than talk," he said, sampling her lips with little sipping kisses. "Touching, tasting, teasing— and those are just the *T* words," he said, lifting his head just enough to give her his naughtiest come-hither smile.

Julia let him shift the mood with his humor. Heaven help her, it felt too good being with him again not to enjoy it for as long as the night would last. She stroked her hands over the smooth, hard muscles of his back and gave him a sassy look. "Are you going to work your way through the entire alphabet, cowboy?"

"Mmm . . ." he growled, nibbling her neck, working his way from her collarbone upward. "Adore . . .

beguile . . ." He kissed a pulse spot as he kneed her legs apart and positioned himself between them. "Consume . . . delight . . . entice . . ." He grazed the butter-soft lobe of her ear with his teeth and whispered the next word in a dark rough chuckle as he eased his shaft into the warm, tight pocket of her womanhood.

Julia's fingers tightened convulsively on the firm, rounded muscles of his buttocks, urging him deeper. The fire that had been banked roared instantly to life inside her, burning away all the questions. For the moment it didn't matter whether she trusted him or not. He was here with her, inside her, and tonight she could hold him and not have to let go.

Seven

The morning of the Wish Foundation picnic dawned clear and warm, Mother Nature taking pity on the people who had endured months of icy roads, frigid winds, and below-zero temperatures. The only clouds in sight were there for artistic effect, gauzy wisps of white to intensify the blue of the sky by contrast.

The annual picnic was being held on the parklike grounds of the toy company Harvey Benton headed in the western suburb of Plymouth, the kind of place where summer days are meant to be whiled away. There was a small pond, picnic shelters, plenty of oak and maple trees for those who preferred shade. A number of carnival rides, including a merry-go-round and a small Ferris wheel, had been set up in a clearing. There was a long row of festively decorated game booths, all run by Wish Foundation volunteers and all guaranteeing winners. Food stands made up another long row and sent the aromas of hot dogs, cotton candy, and popcorn wafting on the summer breeze. At the far end of the little fair a small petting zoo had been set up.

The picnic was not traditionally considered a fund-raising event but a day for the children and families whose lives the foundation sought to brighten. All the activities were free to those wearing blue Wish Foundation badges. The grounds were already crowded with children, many of them in wheelchairs or walking with crutches. Many of them were small for their ages, thin, pale. Some wore baseball caps to shield heads made bald by chemotherapy. They were children who had little joy in their daily existences, children whose lives were marred or would be cut tragically short by illnesses no child should have to know the name of. But on this day they were like any children at a fair. Their laughter rang in the air above the noise and music.

Julia surveyed the scene from the command-post tent with a mix of pleasure and apprehension. There were many more people in attendance who were not associated with the foundation than in most years. Local radio stations had come in and set up booths from which they were doing live broadcasts and giving away an array of prizes. The KORN Aquatennial float was a popular spot, giving away glossy photos of the fiasco in the hospital parking lot. It was very clear to Julia that the extra attention the picnic was garnering was being generated by one thing— S.T.'s challenge to win her heart. And even though the result was going to be increased funds and publicity for the foundation, she was distinctly uneasy about being the reason.

The night spent in S.T.'s arms had only complicated an already complicated situation. She felt as if she was being pulled apart inside, her heart telling her to love him, her brain telling her not to trust him, her conscience needling her about Robert. It wasn't fair of her to string Robert along. She couldn't marry him simply because he was a safe choice; that wouldn't be fair to either of them. But she wasn't looking forward to breaking off with him, because that would leave her even more vulnerable to S.T.'s onslaught.

Try as she might, she couldn't get away from the

fear that S.T.'s renewed interest in her was largely sparked by the challenge between him and Robert, and the challenge of winning over a reluctant lady. Winning was in his blood. He'd hung on to his football career until he could go out a winner, and then he'd shown up on her doorstep. . . . And even if she was able to get past that, the idea of him taking her back to Montana set her stomach churning. He was tired now, in need of rest and a change of scenery, but what would happen when he tired of the peace and quiet? He had lived and thrived in the spotlight for a long time. Could he settle down for good in the middle of nowhere? What if the answer to that was no? Where would that leave her?

A wave of old fears and feelings of abandonment rose up inside her like cold, musty air from a cellar, and she shivered in response. Not that she was even considering marrying him, she hurried to assure herself. She had established a nice life in the Twin Cities. S.T. couldn't just suddenly appear and sweep her off to matrimony and Montana.

"Julia, I cannot believe you volunteered me for this."

The tight, angry male voice was Robert's, but when Julia turned she found herself confronted by a very annoyed clown of the Bozo variety—white makeup, red nose, elaborately painted smile that was pulling downward at the moment. Two conical spires of fluorescent orange hair thrust upward from the top of his head like the horns of some mythical beast. The outfit was completed by a red-and-white polka-dot jumpsuit with ruffled collar and cuffs, and a pair of enormous red shoes that forced him to stand like a duck.

Julia couldn't help her outburst of laughter. The sight of Robert, the proper preppie, in a clown suit was too much. Robert's scowl intensified. He had developed a tic above his right eye and it jerked his furry, stick-on orange eyebrow up and down, giving it the appearance of a live woolly caterpillar glued to his face.

"This is not even remotely humorous," he snapped, stamping one clown shoe in what for him was a show of unbridled fury. "I can't be a clown. I never liked Emmett Kelly. I never liked Ronald McDonald. I never even liked Harpo Marx, and he didn't wear this stupid greasepaint!"

Julia doubled over laughing. She came up holding her stomach, eyes watering, lips twitching. "I'm sorry, Robert," she managed between gasps. "Of course it's not funny." She held her breath until her face turned burgundy as she tried in vain to compose herself. Finally the air exploded from between her lips, making a sound not unlike a Whoopee cushion's.

"Is this what you wanted, Julia?" Robert demanded in low, clipped tones. "For me to make a fool of myself in public?"

"No!" she protested, sobering. "I didn't sign you up to be a clown. I signed you up for the first-aid station."

"Well, guess what?" he queried sarcastically. "Someone made the brilliant suggestion that *every-one* in the first-aid station dress in costume."

"Who? When? I don't know anything about this!"

"Mornin', Legs!" S.T. strode toward them with one of his cat-in-the-cream grins beaming across his lean face. He was in his usual jeans with a tooled belt and silver buckle, but he had traded in his boots for a pair of high-top sneakers and his Western shirt for a royal-blue Wish Foundation T-shirt that made his eyes look bluer than the sky and his shoulders wider than the Hoover Dam. "Howdy, Dr. Bob," he drawled slyly. "Nice outfit. It's you all over."

"You!" Robert fumed, fixing S.T. with a glare. "You're responsible for this, aren't you?"

"Well, I hate to take all the credit," S.T. said with a self-deprecating shrug. "But yeah, I did think it'd be nice for the kids to see doctors in a more enjoyable light for a change." His bandit's grin spread across his face again. "Knowing you were on the list of volunteers was just frosting on the cake."

Julia didn't know whether to scold S.T. or praise him. The idea was a masterstroke. These children had seen far too much of people in lab coats, surgical greens, and nursing whites. Having the doctors and nurses in costume would be a welcome change for them. She turned to Robert with an apologetic look.

"It *is* a good idea," she said. "Just relax, Robert. It's not as if people are going to recognize you."

"Good morning, Storm, Julia, Dr. Bob!" Liz called, waving with her fingers as she walked up to them, her arms laden with costumes, her tiny frame nearly invisible behind the mountain of colorful clothing. She arched a brow as she inspected Robert's appearance, one corner of her lush red mouth tugging upward in a wry smile. "Dr. Bob, this is a new look for you. I had you pictured in the Robin Hood costume, myself. Those little green tights . . ." She narrowed her eyes and pursed her lips. "*Very* sexy."

Robert's blush showed through his greasepaint. He gave Julia a pointed look, which she answered with a rather sickly excuse for a smile. S.T. stepped in and took her by the arm.

"Come along, darlin', we've got things to do. Can't be standing here clowning around all morning."

He tossed a smart-aleck grin back at Robert's scowl, licked the tip of a forefinger and chalked up a point for himself in the air.

Liz patted Dr. Bob's arm consolingly. "Come with me, I'll touch up your eyeliner." Julia watched as her friend steered Robert in the opposite direction. "This could be a really good opportunity for you to explore your inner self," Liz said. "You know, role playing and all like that. I read this article in . . ."

"The guy needs a sense of humor transplant," S.T.

commented as he led Julia past the row of carnival games.

"He can be a little stiff."

"A little? I once knew a cigar-store Indian with more personality."

"Robert is a very nice man," Julia protested, instinctively defending her fiancé.

S.T. cursed himself under his breath as he caught the stubborn set of her chin. He drew her off the path and behind the trunk of a big oak tree for a modicum of privacy. He gave her an apologetic look. "I'm sorry. I shouldn't pick on him like that. It's just that I'm jealous, you know. I can't stand the idea of another man holding you."

Julia felt her temper ebb as she looked up at him. He looked sincerely contrite, an expression that could have won him scores of feminine hearts—blue eyes gazing at her through thick lashes, black hair spilling across his forehead in boyish disarray. "He wasn't holding me last night, was he?" she said.

A slow, sweet smile unfurled across his face and he leaned closer. "No ma'am, he wasn't."

As he settled his lips against hers, a photographer jumped out from behind the next tree and snapped a picture. S.T. sent the man a good-natured grin and a wave as he took Julia by the arm again and led her away. She looked up at him with a troubled expression.

"Goes with the territory, sweetheart," he said gently, sliding his arm around her waist as they walked.

The territory of Storm Dalton, she clarified. How much would he miss that when the spotlight turned elsewhere?

All her questions and misgivings about her own situation with S.T. vanished from sight as they came to the clearing at the end of the row of games. A scaled-down football field had been marked off with white chalk lines on the grass. The field was peopled by big men in purple-and-white jerseys, each surrounded by a swarm of children. Some were giving instructions, some were tossing soft foam footballs into clumsy little arms. One especially enormous blond man was sprawled on the ground not three feet away, having been "tackled" by four little boys. Laughter filled the air, along with shouts of "Good job" and "Way to go."

Julia turned to S.T. with a such a look of pure surprise and happiness, he actually felt his heart skip.

"I got everybody who was still in town for the summer," he said. "I told you they're good ol' boys. They were glad to do it."

Julia looked back out across the field at all the shining young faces gazing up at their heroes and her eyes teared. Many of these children would never have the chance to play football in school, let alone in the NFL, but meeting these men they watched on television and fantasized about would make up for some of the lost dreams.

"You're a wonderful man," she said impulsively, throwing her arms around him for a fierce hug.

"Well now, that's a damn sight better than what you were calling me a week ago." S.T. grinned and wiped a tear from her eye as half a dozen kids came toward him shouting his name. "Hold that thought, honey," he said, dropping a quick kiss on the tip of her nose. "Duty calls."

Julia watched him walk away, herding his flock of admirers toward an unoccupied corner of the miniature football field. This was the S.T. she loved, the man who would run half the day on battle-scarred knees just to please these children. He would let them chase him and knock him down and climb all over him, all the while moving with the lithe grace and finesse of a dancer, but come tomorrow morning he would be groaning and moving with the speed and care of a man twice his age. She knew; she had watched his morning ritual of unsticking rusty joints.

"Cute butt," Vera Creighton murmured conspiratorially as she sidled up to Julia. Her eyes were glued to S.T.'s backside. Julia half expected the woman to start drooling and she felt a profound surge of jealousy rush through her veins. She didn't bother to deny it this time. She might have sicced the woman on him a week ago as a joke, but if Vera made one move toward him today she was going to be in grave danger of losing a few icy blond ringlets.

Vera heaved a dramatic sigh. "He's such a peach. You're a very lucky girl, Julia." She waved a hand at Julia's raised eyebrow. "Oh, Storm told me all about it, darling. How you've stolen his heart. He's just too sweet. You really ought to go to the effort of trying to dress for him, dear."

Julia glanced down at her battered sneakers, baggy khaki shorts and Wish Foundation T-shirt. This was how she always dressed. She thought she had been racing with the trendsetters by tying her hair back with a scarf that matched her T-shirt. Vera, on the other hand, looked like something out of a display at Saks in a vibrant blue sundress with white accessories, including a wide-brimmed straw hat.

"You're giving in easily, Vera," Julia said suspiciously.

"Well, who am I to stand in the way of true love? Besides," Vera said with a throaty chuckle, "Storm introduced me to Lars. Oh, Lars, dear!"

At the sound of his name, the huge blond man rose to his feet with children dangling all over him and lumbered toward them, his arctic-blue eyes boring down on Vera as a smile cracked across his stony face. Vera gave a little squeal of delight.

"Come now, children," she said, her eyes on the man, eating up shoulders as wide as a side-by-side refrigerator. "Let's go get your pictures taken with the great big handsome football star."

Julia watched them go, chuckling. Leave it to S.T. He wouldn't have wanted Vera to harbor bad feelings, so he had fixed her up. And if the searing-hot looks Lars was giving Vera were any indication, S.T. had made his gargantuan friend a very happy man, as well.

Julia spent the entire morning coordinating activities at the football field. The press hovered around the players like flies, most of them swarming around S.T. He tolerated their presence, but made it clear that his first obligation was to spend time with the children, which won him extra points in Julia's heart. She was forced to deal with her share of the media as well, all of them hounding her for word of a winner in the challenge. She gave them nothing but smiles and the standard "No comment."

"When are you going to comment?" Liz asked as they took an afternoon lemonade break in the shade of a big maple tree near the pond.

"No comment," Julia said with a crooked smile. She expected a chuckle from her friend, but she didn't get one. Liz glanced away, fussing with the leather tie of her sandal.

"You love S.T. I think he's the man of your destiny."

"I wish it were that simple. This is all happening so fast. I thought I'd written him off for good. Now . . ." She sighed as she tossed a twig into the pond and watched a mallard paddle over to inspect it. "It's just so risky. I feel like I'm being led by the hand onto a high wire and we're working without a net."

"Isn't Dr. Bob your safety net?"

The Look of Great Wisdom had taken on an extra facet Julia hadn't seen before, but before she could comment on it Liz shook it off, rolling her eyes.

"Love should be easier, you know," she said. "It's like all this courtship stuff was great when people had leisure time. I hardly have time to change my pantyhose these days. How am I supposed to sort through all this romance junk with signals and chemistry and all like that? I was never any good at chemistry, anyway," she confessed, lower lip plumping out in a pout. "In high school I set fire to the lab and had to take an incomplete. I want to go back to the Me Decade. It was easier."

Just as Julia was about to respond, they were descended upon by yet another reporter, who informed her S.T. had just hinted at a fall wedding date.

Julia felt her cheeks flush with instant heat. That bastard. He'd done it again. Just when she thought she might be able to trust him he had to go and open his big mouth. She pushed herself slowly to her feet. "Oh he did, did he? And just where is Mr. Dalton?"

"At the dunk tank," the man supplied.

A nasty smile curled the corners of Julia's mouth. "Oh goody."

She marched toward the dunk tank with a purposeful stride, reporters scurrying after her like rats after the Pied Piper, the pack growing larger as the scent of a possible story caught their noses. The games area had been looking a little deserted, but it quickly filled with people as word spread of a possible confrontation between the hottest couple in the Twin Cities. Julia could hear the crowd gathering around her as she stopped at the rope barrier in front of the tank.

S.T. sat on the bench above the water tank, wearing not much more than a grin. He had stripped down to a pair of electric-blue swim trunks that left little to the imagination except erotic fantasies.

"Hi, baby!"

"Don't you 'hi, baby' me, S. T. Dalton," Julia snapped, grabbing three softballs from the attendant. She fired one at he bull's eye and missed, the ball hitting the canvas curtain with a thud. "How dare you hint that I'm going to marry you this fall!"

Another ball missed its mark, but came closer than the last.

S.T.'s face dropped. "I never hinted anything!"

"Oh great! You told them that right out!"

Whoosh. Thunk!

S.T. braced himself on the seat and glared at her. "I never told anybody anything!"

"Oh right, like you never started this stupid challenge to begin with!" Julia grabbed another set of balls from the attendant without looking at the man. "You know who's going to win this round, cowboy? I am."

Whoosh. Thunk!

S.T. watched her with a mix of anger and admiration. Julia in a rage was a sight to behold. Her dark eyes shone like polished onyx. A color accented the line of her cheekbones and the red in that decadent mouth. She hauled back like an all-star and fired another ball, glancing this one off the target. The crowd gasped.

"Well, I'm gonna win in the end, sweetheart," he taunted, letting his temper take control of his tongue. If she was going to try, convict, and sentence him, he figured he might as well be guilty of something. "I never mentioned a date, but since you've got such a head of steam up about it, do you want to get married sooner than fall?"

"I want to *see* you fall," she snarled, as her willing helper handed her another ball. "Drown, you rat!"

The ball flew, the bell rang, S.T. sucked in a breath and went under. He came up shaking his head, flinging water in all directions. The crowd was roaring. He hiked up his trunks, drawing a chorus of screams from the women in the audience, then pulled himself back onto his perch and shot Julia an infuriating grin.

"Was that a fluke or should the Twins be scouting you out, honey?"

Another fastball flew, the bell rang, S.T. went under.

"How's that for luck, folks?" he called as he hauled himself back onto the bench. He slicked his hair back with both hands. "I'm not only getting a beautiful lady, I'm getting a major-league pitcher!"

The bell rang again.

Julia dunked him twice more. Her arm gave out before her temper did. When she finally stalked away, not even the reporters dared to follow her. She kept her gait just below a jog, not willing to sacrifice any more of her pride by running. Tears of fury stung her eyes, but she refused to let them fall. Damn him! Why did he have to keep making a fool of her? And why did she keep going for the bait? She could have taken a cue from Robert and reacted to the entire challenge by not reacting at all. But she couldn't seem to control her emotions where S.T. was concerned. They lay too close to the surface, were made too volatile by love.

Her step faltered as if the thought had tripped her up physically as well as mentally. She couldn't rein in her responses to S.T., good or bad, because she loved him. Robert hadn't responded to the challenge at all until S.T.'s antics had directly affected him. Was it because he had trusted in her love, or was it because he didn't love her?

She thought of all the events of the past week and further back, taking in her entire relationship with Robert at a glance. They were comfortable together, liked each other, shared a few interests. They had never ignited the kind of blazing sexy chemistry she did with S.T., but Julia had blamed herself and S.T.'s ghost for that. It had never occurred to her that Robert may have drifted into the relationship the same way she had, that he may have seen marriage to her as safe and convenient, that he may have liked her well enough but not loved her, that he may have seen losing this challenge as a graceful way out.

"Oh God," she whispered, leaning against a tree for support as she felt her mental footing give way. "Now I really am working without a net."

S.T. found her at the petting zoo. The animals were getting a break from the earlier heavy traffic, the bulk of the crowd having shifted to the games site. The area was relatively quiet and media free. An old hand at dealing with reporters, S.T. had managed to shake the ones who had been intent on following him. Most of them were off chasing a black pickup down a rural route. There were times when he didn't mind their intrusion on his private life, but this wasn't one of them. He needed to see Julia in private and set her straight on a point or two.

She was keeping a close, watchful eye on a little blue-eyed blonde in a cowgirl outfit. The girl was maybe five, pale and thin, her skin almost translucent due to illness. Crescents of dark purple ringed her eyes. She was busy feeding a handful of hay through the fence to a shaggy Shetland pony. Julia stood a little way down the fence, observing the girl with a wistful expression that vanished the instant she became aware of S.T. The look she shot him could have pierced steel and frozen the fires of hell.

"You've got a hell of an arm, I'll say that for you," he drawled, leaning against the top rail of the makeshift corral. "Can't say much for you as a judge of character, but they don't care about that at the ballpark these days, so I guess you're safe there."

"The pot calls the kettle black," she said sardonically.

"I didn't tell any reporter anything about a fall wedding or any other wedding, for that matter."

Julia glanced at him sideways. He had dressed in his jeans and a fresh T-shirt. The sneakers had been traded in for his battered old boots. His hair was still wet from the dunking she'd given him and he had slicked it back in a way that gave him a hard, hawkish appearance, a look that was enhanced by the steel in his gaze. He was angry with her. Tough.

"Well, I didn't feed them that line," she snapped. "So who's left? Liz?"

"Try your friendly helper at the dunk tank."

"Who?"

"Bozo Bob, Clown Doctor of the North," he said sarcastically. "Jeez, didn't you even notice he was the one feeding you softballs like there was no tomorrow?"

"No," Julia answered in a small voice. She had been so blind with anger she hadn't paid any attention to the people around her. Her focus had been on S.T., the man she loved and wanted to strangle all at once.

"No? Well, I'd say he finally got a couple of licks in." He shifted his stance, turning to face her, one hand on the corral rail, the other propped against his hip. "I'd be a good sport about it except it hurt too damn bad to have you accuse me of something I didn't do."

Julia glanced at her young charge, then turned back to S.T. with a sigh. "I'm sorry, but when that reporter told me you'd hinted at a date, I just saw red. Considering all the other things you've done this week, it certainly didn't seem beyond the realm of possibility. It seems like every time I start believing you're for real, you pull some outrageous stunt. Every time I open a door I cringe, waiting to see a giant plastic farm animal or you in a toga—"

"You don't like my grand gestures?" S.T. said, stunned that he could have been so far off the mark. "I wanted to show you how much I care. I thought if I did it in a big way you'd know I was sincere."

"I know that whenever two or more reporters are gathered around you, the first thing you talk about is that stupid challenge."

He took a step closer, his eyes fixed on hers, his voice a low rumble. "The contest is over as far as I'm concerned. You wouldn't have let me in your bed last night if you didn't love me, Julia. I know you better than that."

"If you know me so well, then how come you keep making me so damn mad?"

"You wouldn't be getting so mad if you weren't trying so hard to fight the fact that you love me." He lifted a hand and brushed his callused fingers over the smooth, soft plane of her cheek. "Would you, Julia?"

Her answer was forestalled as the pony walked away and the little girl looked up at Julia with wide sad eyes.

"I ran out of grass, Julia," she said.

"That's okay, sweetie. We'll get you some more."

"Well, who have we got here?" S.T. asked, hunkering down in front of the urchin.

"This is my friend Angie," Julia said, her voice taking on a completely different tone as she kneeled down beside the little girl. She smiled with a love and gentleness that caught at S.T.'s heart and stirred the desire in him to see her with *their* child. "Angie is staying with me while her mom has a little nap at the first-aid tent. Her mom is going to have a baby in a few weeks."

"Wow," S.T. said, sounding suitably impressed. "Hi, Angie. My name is S.T., but all my best friends call me Storm, so you'd better call me Storm too," he said with a wink.

Angie took in his attire with a critical eye, her gaze homing in on his boots, belt and buckle. "Are you a real cowboy?"

"I sure am. I can ride and rope and wrestle ornery steers—as long as they're not *too* ornery." He scooped the little girl up and perched her on his shoulders, keeping a careful hold on her skinny legs above the tops of her cowboy boots. "Let me tell you about the time I had to rope the biggest bull in all creation with a rope made out of rattlesnakes tied head to tail. . . ."

Julia watched as S.T. gave Angie a piggyback ride around the zoo, making her laugh at his tall tales. Then he supervised her on a pony ride in a shaded ring where five docile ponies tramped around in a circle. By the time the ride was over Angie's mother had returned to retrieve Angie and Julia's temper had been reduced to ashes. Watching S.T. with the child had been enough to dissolve whatever anger had been left in her. He was gentle and attentive and won a month's supply of smiles and giggles from Angie, who didn't have much to smile or giggle about.

He would make a wonderful father.

Will you have my babies, Julia?

As Angie and her mother headed for the games S.T. dropped an arm across Julia's shoulders and walked her away. She let him set the slow pace and choose the direction. They headed away from the noise and people, into the area where many of the helpers had parked their cars.

"Sweet kid," S.T. said. "What's the story there?"

"Leukemia," Julia answered softly, her heart aching instantly at the thought. "It's not responding to treatment."

S.T. winced. "Oh, man. She kept telling me she might get a pony when she turns seven."

Julia shook her head as tears swam up in her eyes. She was too tired to fight them back. She was operating on very little sleep and megadoses of emotion. Given that and a heart too tender to begin with, it was impossible for her to maintain a sense of professional detachment now. Barring a miracle, Angie Stephens wouldn't see her seventh birthday, and knowledge of the impending loss of that one small life suddenly seemed too much to bear. She felt guilty and selfish for letting her own petty problems overwhelm her. What she had to deal with was nothing in comparison to what the Stephens family had to face. Her feet stopped moving and she brought her hands up to cover her face as pain washed through her.

"Hey," S.T. murmured, turning into her. "Come here, sweetheart. You can cry on this shirt if you want to. It's mostly clean."

The words were like a trigger that unleashed the flood of emotion. Julia fell against S.T.'s solid frame and sobbed for all she was worth, soaking the shoulder of his T-shirt, clinging to his steady strength.

"I-I know I'm not supposed t-to get emotionally involved, but I can't help it. She's so sweet an-and she's s-so little. . . ."

"I know, baby. I do it too," S.T. whispered, his lips brushing her temple. "It hurts a lot to think they never get a chance."

His voice went hoarse, then gave out altogether, and Julia looked up to catch him with a sheen of tears in his blue eyes. He held his mouth in a tight line as he dug in his hip pocket for a clean handkerchief, which he lifted to carefully dry her cheeks. Julia's heart swelled with love for him.

"You're the best friend I ever had," she whispered.

The corners of his mouth twitched upward in a sad little smile. "I want to be a lot more than that."

"You know you are. You know I love you." She had expected to feel better saying it, but instead she felt a pressure building in her chest. S.T.'s hand had stilled on her cheek and he stood there looking at her, his expression taut and expectant. "I'm scared, S.T.," she managed to whisper.

S.T. pulled her into his arms and squeezed her tight against him. "I know, baby. I know you're scared to trust me. All I can do is tell you I love you and ask for the time to prove it can last."

Time. Julia didn't want to think about time. She didn't want to think at all. She turned her head and caught S.T.'s mouth with a kiss that was trembling and urgent. He accepted it readily, let her tongue seek out his, groaned as her fingers kneaded the back of his neck. His hands stroked slowly down her back to her hips and he pulled her snugly against the burgeoning evidence of his arousal.

Julia lifted her head, her lids drowsy from the rush of sudden desire. Her lips, puffy and kiss reddened, were slightly parted as she panted for breath. She had managed to lose her scarf and her hair tumbled behind her in a thick curtain made an even more vibrant red by the late afternoon sun. She said nothing. There was no need for words. Their feelings vibrated in the air around them.

S.T. wedged a hand into the pocket of his jeans and fished out a set of keys. Without a word he took Julia's hand and led her to the side entrance of a big RV. Bingo raised his head and woofed at them softly from his post under the camper, then went back to his nap.

"I borrowed this from a friend," S.T. mumbled as he unlocked the door. He stepped up inside and pulled Julia in after him. "I thought it would be a good place to change clothes and sneak into for a little privacy . . ." he said, tossing the keys on the counter and turning to face her, ". . . among other things."

His expression was blatantly sexual, blatantly hungry, the fire in his eyes searing Julia to the core. She wanted to commend him on his ingenuity, but speech seemed well beyond her capabilities at the moment. They stood in the little alcove at the back of the camper, between the bathroom door on the right and a tall cupboard on the left. Julia caught a fleeting impression of clutter and conveniences in the space beyond, but her attention was on S.T.

All predatory male, he came toward her, his gaze locked on hers, his intention clear. The passion that had gathered like summer storm clouds was thick in the air around them. They came together like thunder and lightning, hot, urgent. They kissed greedily, avidly, as if they were trying to consume each other's need. Julia felt S.T. tug her T-shirt up with clumsy hands and dispense with her bra. She fumbled with his shirt, barely breaking the kiss long enough to get it over his head. Her shorts hit the floor. His belt buckle rattled and jeans zipper hissed.

As he took her mouth with his again, S.T. slid his hands down around Julia's hips, his fingers alternately caressing and groping the soft flesh of her buttocks. She reached between them and tried to guide him, her hand closing around the velvet warmth of his shaft. She was empty and aching for him, her need an unbearable molten heat at the core of her. She needed him inside her, around her, touching her, kissing her, confirming their lives and their friendship and their love, giving her something tangible to keep the fear at bay for a little while.

She wrapped her long legs around his hips as he lifted her, and welcomed his thrust with a soft cry that was echoed by his hoarse, masculine voice. They moved together, clung together, each seeking and finding a bliss that blocked out all darkness with its brilliance. Julia wound her arms around S.T.'s shoulders and held on, savoring the feel of his masculine strength throbbing deep within her. S.T. clutched her to him, moaning softly at the exquisite sensation of her woman's body rippling gently around him in the last tremors of orgasm. They were both hot, sweating, gasping for breath as reality returned in the distant sounds of the fair drifting in through the open windows.

S.T. smiled softly as he brushed sweat-damp tendrils of hair from Julia's face. "That brings back memories, doesn't it?"

"Yeah," Julia said, remembering vividly their youthful lovemaking in the fresh straw of an empty box stall at the Lawson County fair. "Do you think Harvey will ground me if I'm a little late getting back?"

"I doubt it," S.T. chuckled wickedly, nipping at her neck. "It's his camper." His expression sobered slowly as he gazed into her eyes. "Can I take this as a sign that you're going to give me a chance?"

Julia's heart was pounding as she stared at him. She had loved him forever. He was the one person on earth who had the power to make her life heaven or hell. She would have been safer pushing him away, but the point was moot. Her heart had already decided to take the first step onto that high wire.

"You've got your chance, S.T.," she murmured. "Please don't blow it this time."

"I won't, baby," he promised softly, eyes locked on hers. He lifted a hand and traced an *X* over her breastbone. "Cross my heart."

Eight

Julia stared at the dress spread across her bed and nibbled her lower lip. Liz had talked her into it. It really wasn't her style at all—too flamboyant—but then people weren't allowed to go to gala fund-raisers in ripped jeans and T-shirts depicting cartoons of body organs at the beach. It was gorgeous, no question—a simple, figure-skimming, knee-length sheath of black silk with a shoulder-hugging portrait neckline of shimmering black satin. The question was, did she have any underwear good enough to put on beneath it?

Tightening the belt on her robe she went to her dresser to begin the search. She had meant to go shopping for some silky, sexy stuff during the week, but it seemed her every moment had been filled. Between work and S.T. there had been no time for anything except fretting—first about how to tell Robert it was over between them, then about what she would do now that Robert was no longer in the picture.

As it had turned out, breaking up with Robert hadn't been all that difficult. In fact, it had seemed remarkably, sadly easy for them to sit down and discuss the fact that the relationship they had intended to commit their lives to was over. It had frightened Julia a little to think they had each been willing to settle for a marriage based on something less than true love. But what frightened her more was to think of the love she felt for S.T. and to realize the true enormity of the commitment he was asking of her.

He was asking her to trust him when the road of their past was littered with the charred wrecks of their previous relationships. He was asking her to give up the safe, sound life she had carved out for herself, to leave her friends behind and follow him to a place she associated with a largely miserable youth. He was asking her to give him her heart, whole and healed, and risk having it broken again, and heaven help her, she wasn't sure she could do it.

S.T. had spent the week wooing her in sweet ways, giving up on the grand gestures he had thought would win her heart. He had taken her for a moonlight canoe ride and picnic on Long Lake, they had gone for walks in the woods, spent time just looking at the stars while lying on an air mattress in the bed of his pickup. It had all been wonderfully romantic, especially the long, slow hours of lovemaking. No man had ever been able to make her feel so feminine or fragile or blissful in bed as S.T. Their chemistry was perfect. Julia should have been ecstatic that he had finally asked her to marry him, but she was terrified instead.

Every time S. T. brought up the subject of moving to Montana to his ranch, Julia's stomach wound itself into a knot no Boy Scout could untie. He had been patient with her, but Julia knew her reluctance was hurting him. He may have been all grown up and gorgeous on the outside, but inside he still had the tender heart of the boy she'd know in Muleshoe.

Julia's hands stilled, wrist deep in lingerie, as her fingertips brushed across something in the bottom of the drawer. Her airline ticket to California. She pulled out the packet, disentangling it from the stranglehold of panty hose and bra straps, and stared at it long and hard. The flight was to leave Sunday noon. Tomorrow. High noon. She hadn't talked about the trip all week, hadn't once mentioned it to S.T. Neither had she canceled her vacation time from the hospital, or the flight, for that matter. She had studiously avoided thinking about it. Two weeks ago she had been hanging on, counting the minutes until she could escape. And now . . .

"Thank God you're not dressed yet!" Liz burst into the room, a dramatic flash of color in gold tights and a tunic of hectic neon-colored blocks. Her arms were weighed down by shopping bags, which she hefted onto the bed. "You can't put that dress on over any piece of underwear you own."

"Why?" Julia asked, slipping the airline ticket back under her briefs. "Will there be a chemical reaction?"

"I won't let you out of the house, that's why," Liz said, dumping the contents of one bag onto the bedspread. "What if you were in an accident and had to be taken to the hospital and they saw you were wearing cotton underwear?"

Julia slanted her a look. "Gee, that *would* be terrible. I'd probably die of embarrassment, if not of my wounds."

Liz shook her head and clucked her tongue as she sorted through the pile of new underthings, going on as if Julia hadn't spoken. "Then someone would recognize you and say, 'Hey, isn't she Julia McCarver, the one who's dating Storm Dalton? Isn't her roommate the one who runs The Glamourama?' And then my career would be over."

Julia lifted a pair of black lace French-cut panties and raised an eyebrow. "And if I'm in an accident while wearing this stuff people will merely think I was moonlighting as a hooker. I see. That's a great improvement."

"They'll think you're in love with a famous sexy

cowboy. And if they read the labels, they'll know where women who date famous sexy cowboys shop." She gave a shrug and a cheeky grin. "And then I'll get a big raise because of all the new customers and everybody will have nice underwear and live happily ever after."

"Really, Liz, you ought to run for president," Julia said dryly as she dangled a garter belt from her fingertips. "You could run on a foundation garments platform."

Liz lifted her nose in the air and gave a delicate sniff. "Make jokes if you will, but I know a certain cowboy who's going to cast his vote in my favor when he sees you tonight." She glanced at the big scuba diver's watch on her wrist and muttered something in Spanish as she scooped up the rest of the shopping bags and hurried toward the door. "I've got to hit the shower. Don't you dare leave before I see you and make sure you're not wearing sneakers or earrings with dog heads on them."

"Yes, Mother." Julia chuckled. Where would she be without Liz? she wondered as she turned toward the mirror holding a black strapless bra up against her chest. Her smile faded slowly and her eyes grew wide.

She'd be in Montana with no friends and cotton underwear and a man she loved too much for her own good.

The downtown hotel where the Wish Foundation ball was being held was new and lavish, a testimony to the growing prosperity and established sophistication of the Twin Cities. The ballroom was richly appointed with white moiré silk on the walls and enormous chandeliers made of crystal beads that sparkled like diamonds against the high ceiling. The pillars and wainscoting were cherry wood with a patina that glowed like satin in the soft light. One hundred round tables had been draped in white linen and set with centerpieces of fresh flowers. The dance floor shone like water in the moonlight.

It was an impressive setting with an equally impressive crowd. Everyone who was anyone in the metro area was there. Businessmen, politicians, and celebrities, as well as the volunteers who donated their time and talents year-round to the cause. Julia had never seen so many tuxedos in one place. And dotted among the elegant black-and-white suits were gowns in soft pastels and dramatic jewel tones.

Julia felt a little like an oversize Cinderella, not quite comfortable in her chic dress and high heels. She towered over the other women and many of the men, and she felt a little naked in the off-the-shoulders dress. Liz had performed an act of magic on her wild mane, sweeping it up into an artless style that was mysteriously secured with a minimum of hairpins. The weight of it and the fear that the pins would fall out were giving her a stiff neck.

S.T. had donned the requisite tux, but his jacket had a subtle Western cut that emphasized his broad shoulders. Standard patent-leather shoes had lost out to a pair of polished black cowboy boots. The cummerbund had been abandoned in favor of a narrow black leather belt with a tasteful sterling buckle. He looked rakish and sexy and Julia realized with no small amount of embarrassment that she was getting goose bumps just holding his hand.

" . . . and Julia, dear, you look lovely," Harvey Benton said, bestowing on her a benevolent smile as he turned his attention away from S.T. "Have I thanked you yet tonight for bringing Storm back into our fold just in the nick of time? You can't imagine the extra money we've made because of the two of you."

Julia tried to swallow down the sour-tasting knot of apprehension that was lodged at the back of her throat and mustered a smile of thanks for Harvey. He meant well. He had no idea the sight of the press people roaming the crowd or the size of the crowd itself made her queasy. Apparently S.T. had no idea either. He slid an arm around her waist and grinned for a photographer just as the flash blinded them.

"They're out in force tonight," she muttered as S.T. guided her toward the dance floor.

"Just ignore them, honey," he said, drawing her into his arms, his body swaying gently to the music.

"It's kind of hard to ignore a zillion-watt light going off in your face every five minutes."

"Yeah, well, I guess I'm kind of used to it."

Julia said nothing, but her hand tightened on his and she stepped a little closer to him, seeking solace in his masculine strength and warmth. She wanted to be close to him, needed to be close to him, and a cynical little voice inside her told her to get close to him while she still could.

"I feel like everyone in the place is staring at us," she said, sneaking a glance at the crowd that milled at the edge of the dance floor. Dozens of eyes followed their every move. It brought back memories of being the tallest girl in school, feeling as conspicuous as a giant at a dwarf festival. The two weeks of S.T.'s challenge were over tonight and everyone in town who could afford a ticket or finagle a press pass was there to observe the outcome.

"It's you, you know," S.T. murmured, his lips brushing the shell of her ear as he maneuvered them away from the watchful eyes of the crowd. "They can't resist you. They're like a bunch of fireflies attracted to a brilliant light."

He pressed a soft kiss to her temple and let his right hand trace the womanly curve of her waist and hip through the clinging fabric of her dress. "I love the way you look in this dress. Like a movie star. Like a princess." His husky voice dropped a notch as he rubbed the tip of his nose against hers and looked her in the eyes, his gaze warm and intimate. "I bet I'll love the way you look out of this dress too."

He leaned back and gave a hoarse chuckle at the blush that crept up from the tops of Julia's breasts to the tips of her ears. It never failed to surprise him how unconscious Julia was of her own beauty, or to touch him how unsure she was of her appeal. She stood there in his arms, gorgeous enough to knock the most jaded of men off their feet, and she was blushing because he'd given her a compliment.

In many ways she was still that uncertain girl whose father had left her behind. Every time he caught a glimpse of that girl in her wide dark eyes the love he felt for her was like a fountain, overflowing from his heart and spreading through him in tingling streams. He wanted to sweep her away, off the dance floor, off the planet if possible, and have her entirely to himself, but he checked the urge even as he checked the exit routes from the ballroom. He wanted Julia to go away with him, to commit herself to him, but she had to make the decision herself. He couldn't force her to love him enough to trust him.

He watched her cast a wary glance at a roaming photographer and wondered how long it would be before she could believe in him again, wholly, without looking for ulterior motives in his actions, without holding back some part of her heart. The past week had been wonderful, the time they'd spent together special, the sex fantastic, but it had all been given a slightly gray cast by Julia's hesitancy. She tried not to let it show, but he could feel it as easily as if it had been his own misgiving. They were too in tune for him not to.

He pulled her a little closer as the music slowed and the sounds of a bluesy saxophone drifted on the air like smoke. He turned her deftly and dodged the photographer with a smooth move that landed them in the center of the mob of dancers.

"Liz came alone?" he asked. *Bide your time, S.T. Don't push.*

"Mmm. She decided to take a page from Vera

Creighton's book and do a little trolling for the man of her destiny. Personally, I think she's gone over the edge with this marriage obsession."

"The guy with the MBA and the BMW didn't work out?"

"No. Turned out he only wanted to sell her an annuity. She thinks maybe her signals are getting weak or something."

"Gee, I don't know," S.T. said as he caught sight of his little spy dancing with Dr. Bob. "Looks to me like she's doing all right."

"Liz and Robert?" Julia let loose a laugh that drew looks and smiles from the dancers around them. "I don't think so."

"Why not?"

"Well, because," she sputtered, the answer seeming too obvious for words, "she thinks he's boring and he thinks she's a flake. They're about as mismatched as fire and ice."

S.T. conceded the point with a tip of his head. "Still, stranger things have happened."

Vera Creighton and Lars came dancing by at that point, gazing intently into each other's eyes, like contestants in a staring marathon. Vera was resplendent in a white ankle-length gown with a slit skirt that threatened to expose everything but her date of birth. Lars was nearly bursting the seams of a tuxedo jacket that was Vikings purple. He wore no shirt, but a gold-lamé vest and a matching bow tie that hung above a wedge of hairy pectorals.

Julia's gaze drifted from one unlikely couple to the other. Lars and Vera? Liz and Robert? Could they possibly . . . ? Nah . . . "Didn't anyone tell Lars this is *black* tie?"

"Do *you* want to be the one?" S.T. asked, arching a brow as his gaze traveled up to the top of the lineman's blond head.

"I guess not." Julia watched in amazement as the

couple shuffled away. "I'd say they're proof positive that love conquers all—including bad taste."

"And past mistakes?" S.T. murmured.

All the teasing good humor had suddenly gone out of his expression. Julia looked into his eyes and felt the need, the regret, and his love for her. She lifted her hand from his shoulder and brushed her fingertips along the lean hard line of his jaw. "I love you."

"But you still don't trust me."

"You said you'd give me time," Julia said, tensing in his arms. "Did that mean I could have all the time I wanted until the contest was over?"

S.T.'s face darkened. He glanced away from her, jaw working as he struggled with his temper. When he turned back to her he spoke through his teeth. "Dammit, Julia, I told you, the contest is over as far as I'm concerned."

"You're just waiting for me to publicly declare you the winner, is that it?"

"That is not it."

Another flash went off in their faces and a small tape recorder was thrust between them.

"Hey, Storm, is this a victory dance?" The reporter's voice came from somewhere behind the glare.

Julia heaved a sigh and tried in vain to pull out of his grasp. S.T. held firm. He flashed a practiced smile for the reporter, but muttered a nasty word between his teeth as he felt Julia stiffen even more in his arms. The trust he had worked all week to gain was fast vaporizing in the afterglow of flash bulbs. He could see more uneasiness and wariness creep into Julia's expression as the press closed in on them. He cursed himself for ever coming up with the idea of the challenge. It had seemed a stroke of genius at the time, but if one more person tried to crown him the victor tonight he was going to lose her altogether.

"Sorry fellas, this cowboy doesn't kiss and tell," he said.

A barrage of questions hit them as S.T. steered Julia toward the sidelines.

"Meet me on the other side of that exit door in five minutes," he murmured in her ear, his gaze directing her toward the most remote corner of the ballroom.

Julia gave him an incredulous look. "What? No! I'm not going anywhere with you."

S.T.'s eyes were like blue steel as he leaned close. "Meet me on the other side of that door or I'll throw you over my shoulder and carry you out of here in front of God and everybody."

Julia wasn't about to call his bluff. She had no doubt he would do exactly what he said. Visions of her fanny plastered across the front page of the Sunday-morning *Star Tribune* flashed through her head, making her vaguely dizzy. She gave him a scathing look, crossing her arms beneath her breasts and tightening her mouth into a long, thin line.

S.T. flashed her a roguish grin and flicked a finger down the slope of her nose. "I thought you'd see this my way." His gaze dropped meaningfully to her décolletage and his voice dropped to a hoarse rumble. "Remember that pose for later. I can't wait to see it without the dress. Ooo la la."

Julia gasped as she caught a view of her own cleavage, breasts threatening to spill up over the satin band of her neckline. She dropped her arms and hauled one fist back, intent on punching the man a good one. Chuckling like a maniac, S.T. dodged the blow and moved on through the crowd as if he was headed for the bar to get them some refreshments.

"Oooooh, that man!" Julia snapped. A pin shot out of her hair and tendrils of red silk drifted down along one side of her neck.

"I second that," Liz said. She was fuming as she took up a militant stance beside Julia, hands on the curvy hips revealed by her red dress, black eyes glittering dangerously, one red shoe tapping out a staccato beat against the polished wood floor. "Men. They are impossible!" she spat, her accent thickening noticeably with her rising temper.

Julia followed her gaze across the room to where Robert stood, deep in conversation with his stockbroker. "Are we talking about Robert?" she asked with disbelief. "Is there something going on with you two?"

Liz gave a laugh of outrage and hysteria. "Of course not! How could he possibly be the man of my destiny? It would be more exciting to watch golf on television than to spend time with him. I would rather watch people sleep. He brings new meaning to the word *boring*."

He turned then and came toward them, a look of determination drawing his brows together and turning down the line of his mouth. He nodded to Julia, but never took his eyes off Liz, who had turned her head to gaze somewhere else, affecting her Look of Great Boredom.

"I believe you still owe me a dance," he said. His voice was calm but tension thrummed in the undercurrents.

"Really? I'd lost track. Perhaps you should dance with your stockbroker instead."

"My stockbroker is a man."

Liz lifted one dainty shoulder in a shrug of supreme indifference as the band struck up a tune with a Latin beat. She started to turn away from him. Robert reached out, snagged her wrist, and pulled her back. Liz gave a little squeak of surprise as she landed smack against his chest. Their gazes locked and heated visibly to a temperature that could have melted synthetic fabrics.

"Have you ever done the lambada?" she asked breathlessly.

Julia looked on in stunned amazement as they stepped out onto the dance floor together. Liz and Robert?

The flash of a camera nearby broke her trance and she glanced at the slim gold watch Liz had loaned her. Her five minutes were up. As yet another reporter drew a bead on her and headed her way she set off, winding through the crowd, crouching to keep her head below the others. By the time she reached the exit she had a crick in her neck and had lost two more hairpins.

She pushed open the exit door and slipped through it into a brightly lit service stairwell, letting out a little yelp of surprise as S.T. pulled her into his arms and backed her up against the door. Her lips parted in a gasp as her bare shoulders came into contact with the cold steel door, an action S.T. took as an invitation. He kissed her fervently, hungrily, his solid body pressing into hers. When he finally raised his head all she could do was look at him and blink dazedly.

He drew the back of his hand across his mouth and gave her a rakish grin. "I've been wanting to do that all night."

"Well, gee, don't let me stop you," Julia said weakly.

S.T.'s eyes darkened to the blue of midnight. His voice was like the brush of velvet against her nerve endings. "Do you want to stop me, Julia?"

She had the feeling he was asking about something more than the kiss, but she wasn't ready to answer that question yet. There was no avoiding the flash of pain in his expression when she didn't respond, but it disappeared so quickly she almost wanted to believe she had imagined it.

"Come on," he said taking her by the hand and tugging her toward the stairs.

"But the ball—"

"Legs," he said, tossing her a sly smile that sent shivers of anticipation racing over her. "We're gonna have us our own ball. In private."

Julia told herself she should dig her heels in and refuse, but that was just some of her leftover pique trying to reassert itself. The truth of the matter was, she wanted to be alone with him. When they were alone she could pretend there were no problems. When they were alone she never thought about the challenge, didn't dwell on S.T.'s love of the limelight.

Minutes later, after climbing several flights of the service stairs and sneaking a ride in a freight elevator, they arrived at the door of a suite on the top floor. S.T. produced a room key from his trouser pocket, flashing it before her eyes with a wicked, knowing look, like a magician pulling coins out of thin air. He pushed the door open and motioned her inside with a deep formal bow.

Bingo greeted them with a soft woof, but didn't bother to rouse himself from an overstuffed off-white sofa in the sitting area. Julia ignored him as she stepped out of her shoes and turned around in a circle, marveling at the room. The color scheme was a combination of dark green and shades of beige, accented with subtle touches of mauve and burgundy. The decor was a rich blend of traditional and contemporary, warm, dark cherry wood and cool, light carpeting as plush as new snow. The flower arrangement on the sofa table looked as if an entire garden had gladly sacrificed itself for the honor.

"Just another place to slip away to for a little privacy?" she said dryly.

"I like to be ready for anything," S.T. said as he tugged his bow tie loose and unfastened the top two studs of his shirt.

"I like your style, cowboy."

Julia padded noiselessly across the rug to a set of French doors that opened onto a small balcony. She swung the doors open and stepped out into the warm summer night. The lights of the city spread out below them, giving the feeling that they had somehow raised themselves above the stars. Sounds of traffic drifted up like distant music.

"You didn't seem to think much of my style downstairs," S.T. said. He leaned a shoulder against the door frame and watched her as she moved to the railing.

"You know I don't like the attention from the press. It makes me nervous, all those eyes watching every move we make—"

"Wondering if I'm trying to impress you or them?"

She didn't answer him, but devoted a long moment to staring down at the fingernails Liz had polished red for her. They looked as foreign to her as if someone had glued rose petals to the ends of her fingers. From the corner of her eye she saw S.T. step up to the railing to her left, his expression tense, gaze fixed on her.

"You *really* think I'm that shallow?"

"I don't think you're shallow." She glanced at him sideways and gave him a lopsided, hesitant smile. "I think you're a ham."

S.T. laughed softly, the corners of his eyes crinkling. "Well, you've got me pegged there, sweetheart. I guess I've always been a ham with the press. That just seemed the smartest way to play it." He sobered as he moved closer. "But we're all alone now. There's no one here to impress but you, baby."

He stepped behind her, his arms sliding around her waist. He rested his chin on her bare shoulder. "I spent most of my life trying to win attention from anybody who would look, but that's all done now. All I want is you."

"I want that to be true, S.T.," Julia said, her voice soft and wistful. She tilted her head to the side, giving his lips access to the long column of her throat. He took advantage, nuzzling aside the strands of hair that had escaped her elegant coif and caressing the ivory skin with the softest of kisses.

"It is true," he whispered, each word a brush of his lips against her, a warm breath that seemed to slide right down the front of her dress. "All I want is you, the ranch, peace and quiet. . . ."

"But for how long?" she asked, finally giving voice to the fear.

"Forever."

He turned her in his arms and studied her face in the pale amber light. She looked young and vulnerable, like a little girl who had been caught playing dress-up with her mother's things. The sophisticated hairstyle was in disarray. She stared up at him, her eyes like pools of obsidian in her face, her lips softly parted.

"Is it me you doubt, baby?" he asked softly, his eyes narrowed as he tried to read her innermost fears and feelings. "Or is it yourself? Are you afraid you won't be enough to keep me down on the farm? Is that what this is really all about?"

Julia's eyes widened. She started to deny it, but the words wouldn't come. Her breath caught in her throat as her other fears were peeled aside and she saw the deepest truth that had been hidden beneath them. She had good reason to doubt S.T., but beneath that distrust was a doubt she hadn't faced in years: that she wasn't pretty enough or smart enough or exciting enough, that her love wouldn't mean enough and she would be left alone again.

"I'm not your daddy," S.T. murmured. "And I'm no longer some kid afraid of commitment. I'm a man, Julia, and I'm tired of playing games. I love you and I want you. Tonight. Every night. Forever and ever, amen."

He certainly looked like a man who meant what he said. In this light he looked older, tougher, the lines of his face more deeply drawn.

"Show me," she whispered. Her heart was pounding as she leaned against him, her hands flat on the lapels of his jacket. "Show me, S.T."

"It'd be my pleasure, ma'am," he said with a soft smile and a twinkle in his eye.

Julia expected him to kiss her, to sweep her off her feet and carry her to the bedroom. Instead, he took

her by the hand and led her back inside. Bingo
followed them to the bedroom door with a hopeful
look, but was sent back to the sitting room. Julia
watched the big dog slink away.

"Poor Bingo. He only wants to be with us."

"Let him get his own girl," S.T. said, pulling the
bedroom door shut. "Besides, I think what he really
wants has less to do with us and more to do with
food."

"Food?"

He turned her by the shoulders and Julia gave a
little exclamation of surprise. The room was as beau-
tifully appointed as the other. There was a king-size
bed covered with a dark-green spread, the headboard
lined with plump floral-print pillows. Brass wall
lamps on either side cast the room in a warm,
intimate glow. Another set of French doors opened
onto another small balcony that offered a slightly
different view of the city. On the balcony was a small
round table draped in white linen and set with silver
and china. There were candles waiting to be lit and a
serving cart loaded with glass-covered dessert trays.

"That dog is just a fiend for cheesecake," S.T. said
as he struck a match and set it to the wicks of the
white tapers.

"S.T.," Julia whispered, enchanted as the candle-
light twinkled off the crystal. "You did all this for
me?"

He took her in his arms, his body swaying to the
soft romantic music drifting out of the portable
cassette player on the second tier of the cart. "Everything I do, I do for you, baby."

She dropped her head to his shoulder and danced
with him in silence while she blinked back a sudden
sheen of sentimental tears. He was that sweet. She
probably could have asked him for the moon and
he would have gone off and found a friend with a
space ship he could borrow.

"Pretty sure you'd get me up here, weren't you,

cowboy?" she said, teasing lights dancing in her dark eyes as she raised her head.

"That's me," he grinned. "Cock sure."

Julia groaned. "I wouldn't touch that with a ten-foot pole."

"Well, shoot, honey, that's gonna put a damper on the rest of the night."

She wriggled out of his grasp and danced away from him, giggling. "You're impossible!"

"Naw, I'm not impossible," he drawled, stalking her around the table with a devilish gleam in his eyes. "Tough, maybe. Hard, definitely. Wanna see?"

Julia ducked around the serving cart, pretending indifference. "No, I don't want to see," she said primly, stroking a finger over the cover on a wedge of carrot cake. "I want to eat."

"Oh, I like the sound of that even better."

"Carrot cake," she specified. "Cheesecake. Chocolate fudge torte." She arched a brow. "All desserts?"

S.T. tilted his head and spread his arms wide. "You know my motto: Life's too short. Eat dessert first." He waggled his brows at her lasciviously. "Come here, my little cupcake."

Julia burst into giggles as he lunged for her and wrapped her up in his arms. Her struggles were a token effort at best, designed more for snuggling against him than for escaping. As his mouth found hers, he tunneled his fingers into her hair. The last of the hairpins dropped free and Julia's long mane cascaded down her back like a fiery waterfall.

Slowly S.T. sank one knee to the seat of a chair, his mouth moving seductively down Julia's throat to the curve of her shoulder and the upper slope of her breast. Julia gasped as he peeled the bodice of her dress down. She had been too wrapped up in what his mouth was doing to realize his hands had been busy with her zipper.

She pressed her arms against her sides to keep the dress from falling off, unwittingly plumping her breasts up for S.T.'s delectation. He groaned and murmured heartfelt words of appreciation for both her body and her choice of lingerie. He watched in rapt fascination as her nipples beaded with arousal, then leaned forward and stroked his tongue across one peak that strained the black silk fabric of her bra.

Julia moaned and brought her hands up to tangle her fingers in his hair and press him to her breast. Sensation swirled through her as S.T.'s mouth closed over her once again and he suckled her, then drew back and blew gently across the wet fabric.

"S.T., please," she breathed, reaching up between them to peel the silken cup away. "Please."

S.T. cupped the soft ivory globe gently in one hand, rubbing his thumb slowly back and forth across the dusky mauve tip. He looked up at her face, her parted lips, her eyes heavy-lidded with desire. She wanted him. In all the years, that had never changed. She wanted him, needed him with her body. He only hoped she would see that she needed him with her heart and soul as well, because if she didn't his life wouldn't be worth anything. The love he felt for her bordered on desperation. She was a part of him, the best part of him. He would do anything to prove that to her, but ironically everything he had done so far had worked against him. The small things had failed to convince her, the grand gestures had failed utterly. The only time he felt he had all of her was when they made love.

"Come on, baby," he murmured, rising. "Let's go inside. We need a bed for what I've got in mind."

Nine

Julia awoke as the first pink light of dawn tinted the glass of the French doors. S.T. was dead to the world, sprawled on his stomach, taking up two-thirds of the bed. His face was turned toward her, brow furrowed as if he was working very hard at sleep. His black hair was endearingly rumpled and the dark-green sheet was riding low on his hips, leaving his muscular back exposed down to the rise of his buttocks. Julia studied him for several moments, contemplating what it would be like to wake up next to him for the next few decades.

Her stomach fluttered at the thought, but the butterflies were of hope and anticipation instead of fear. Sometime during the long night of loving she had decided to trust him. He had made a very convincing argument, she remembered, her mouth curving in a secretive woman's smile as her body flushed and warmed in all the tender spots he had nuzzled and kissed. Her fingers curled into the drift of bedclothes and one hand came away with a scrap of black lace. Her garter belt. That and the stockings had been the last to go, S.T. fulfilling Liz's prediction. He had indeed appreciated her taste in lingerie and hadn't been at all shy about telling her so.

The memories flashed through her mind like bits of film. S.T.'s big hands bracketing her hips as she, still in the garter belt and hose, straddled him. His mouth burrowing through the curtain of her hair to find her nipple. Her back arched, hips straining against his, head thrown back. Hot, exciting, uninhibited, as it always was with them. Bodies moving in sinuous synchronization. Hearts thundering in unison. The end coming for them both in an explosion of feeling that went on and on. S.T. enfolding her in his arms in a crushing embrace and rocking her as he whispered over and over that he loved her, that he needed her.

The night had stretched on with an endless quality. At some point they had dragged the serving cart into the room and refueled on the desserts, feeding each other bits of cake with their fingers, laughing and giggling and snatching kisses in between bites. The need for nourishment had quickly given way to other needs, the air becoming charged with the electricity of desire as fingers lingered on lips and gazes caught and held. Julia blushed at the memory of their abandon. S.T. had found uses for frosting no pastry chef had ever dreamed of.

He grumbled now in his sleep and changed position, claiming yet another section of mattress. Julia contemplated waking him up with kisses, but she dismissed the idea. As appealing as it was, she wanted this time alone with her thoughts. She was on the verge of a momentous decision. She needed to go over it in her mind again, let it settle in.

She was going to marry S.T. Dalton.

She slipped from the bed before S.T. could push her out, and shrugged into the tuxedo shirt he had abandoned on the floor. She pulled the drapes closed across the French doors and padded silently out into the sitting room with a plate of cheesecake for Bingo. The big dog was lying on his back on the sofa with his front paws curled against him, back legs spread wide. His tongue hung out the side of his mouth. He was snoring. Julia shook her head and picked up the phone to call for room service.

After a long, hot shower she slipped back into S.T.'s pleated shirt and went to the door toweling her hair to see if the coffee had arrived. Awaiting her was a serving cart with a carafe each of coffee and orange juice, a china plate of artistically arranged fruits, and a linen-lined basket brimming with muffins. The Sunday-morning *Star Tribune* was neatly folded and tucked beside the plate. Rosebuds and baby's breath stood in a crystal vase.

"Classy joint," she murmured, wheeling the tray inside.

The aroma of hot muffins roused Bingo, and he rolled off the sofa and ambled over, sniffing. Julia tossed him a bran muffin as she plucked the paper to check the headlines.

STORM SWEEPS CHALLENGE—NETWORK CONTRACT TOO?

She actually felt her heart stop as she read the bold type. Below it was a full-color photograph that took up half the page, of herself and S.T. smiling at each other as they danced. The story ran in a column down the side, the smaller headline reading DALTON LANDS LADY AND COOL TWO MIL.

Her knees wobbled and she collapsed into an armchair, clutching the paper so hard her knuckles went white.

The sun is certainly shining on ex–pro quarterback Storm Dalton these days. At last night's Wish Foundation benefit ball it was more than apparent that he had won the heart of local trauma nurse Julia McCarver after two weeks of high-profile wooing that had the entire metro area involved. Less publicized have been the hush-hush talks between NBC and Dalton's agent, Davis Williams. Late last night a network source claimed Dalton is reportedly being offered "some-

*thing in the neighborhood of two million [dollars]"
to do color commentary for NFL games. Neither
Dalton nor his agent has been reached for comment.*

The rest of the column melted together in a blur as
tears brimmed up in Julia's eyes. He hadn't said a
word. Not one word. Not even a hint.

*. . . All I want is you and the ranch and peace
and quiet. . . .*

Two million dollars. Network television. S.T., who
loved the limelight, who admitted to playing up for
the press, who was always ready with a grin and a
snappy comment. He would be perfect for the job,
Julia reflected, her emotions shorting out, leaving
her numb. He was handsome, popular, witty in a wry,
down-home way that would appeal enormously to a
television audience. She could see it all now. He was
already doing commercials, next would be the games,
then cameo spots on Bob Hope specials and appearances on *The Tonight Show* and *Letterman*. He
would be an even bigger celebrity than he had been
during his heyday as a quarterback.

And where would that leave her? On a ranch
outside Muleshoe, Montana, waiting for him to come
home.

Julia's capacity for calm, rational thought was
quickly trampled by old fears. They came charging
out of her subconscious, a stampede of memories of
loneliness and inadequacy and abandonment. The
feelings assaulted her, bombarded her from all sides.
How could she possibly hold S.T.'s attention over two
million dollars and a chance to become a star all over
again? Her love had never been enough to hold him
in the past, and the competition hadn't been nearly
so stiff. He had left her every time—for the chance to
play big-time college ball, for the chance to play pro
ball, for the chance to extend his career.

She hurled the newspaper aside, sending Bingo

scurrying from his perch on the sofa. She ignored the dog's wounded look and pressed her hands over her face in a vain attempt to stem the flow of tears. What was she supposed to do now? S.T. claimed he loved her, needed her. He had asked for her trust, but he had kept this little tidbit of news a secret from her. Why?

Answers chased one another around and around in her mind like squirrels racing up and down the trunk of a tree. She thought about confronting S.T. with the paper and demanding an explanation, but dismissed the idea just as quickly. The state of mind she was in, he would probably be able to feed her any cock-and-bull story and convince her to stay with him. Not because she was that gullible, but because she wanted that badly for it to be true. She wanted him to love her, to need her, to want to spend the rest of his life with her in the middle of nowhere. She wanted it so badly she was aching with it.

God, what kind of desperate creature was she that she would go on loving a man who broke her heart time and again, that she would agree to marry a man she didn't love to escape the possibility of being hurt, that she would go back to S. T. Dalton yet again only to have him play her for a fool?

She pushed herself to her feet and looked at her reflection in the mirror on the wall. Her hair was a wild tangle of wet red ropes. S.T.'s shirt swallowed up her body, making her look boyish, flat-chested, and thin. Her eyes and mouth dominated her face like the cheap paintings of sad-eyed children her Aunt Clarisse had hung in the downstairs hall.

Who was this person looking back at her? Was she still, as S.T. had suggested, the little girl whose father had left her, or was she the self-sufficient woman who had carved out a nice, safe life for herself? Was she still S.T.'s little lovesick shadow or . . . what?

Whatever the answer was, it was a cinch she wasn't

going to find out standing in the middle of Storm Dalton's hotel room.

The house was quiet and empty as she packed. She gave no thought as to where Liz might be on a sunny, quiet Sunday morning. She merely thanked her lucky stars no one was there to question her or try to change her mind. Her thoughts were racing ahead to California and escape. She needed to get away, needed time to think without S.T.'s intoxicating influence swaying her. She had the ticket, had the time off, motive, means, and opportunity. In an hour she would be winging her way to the West Coast. By the end of the day she would be sitting on a beach contemplating the meaning of her life. Maybe, if she was very, very lucky, she would be able to figure out who she was and what she was going to do with herself sometime in the next two weeks.

She paid no attention to what she was packing, throwing in a dozen pairs of panties but no socks, a beach cover-up but no swim suit, a wool dress, sandals, two ski sweaters, and three old nursing uniforms she hadn't worn in five years. All that mattered was that she was packing. That was what people going on vacation did.

She dug her plane ticket out of her lingerie drawer and stuck it in her purse, then checked her reflection in the mirror, as if it might tell her whether or not she had forgotten anything important. She had thrown on a pair of jeans with the knees out and a T-shirt that depicted a cartoon of cats performing neurosurgery. Her hair had dried during the ride from the downtown hotel in a cab doing seventy with the windows wide open. It stood out around her head in a wild cloud of flame. She grabbed a pair of white pantyhose out of the drawer, hacked one leg off with nail scissors and used the detached nylon to tie her mane back into a loose ponytail.

She nearly made a clean getaway. Nearly. Suitcase in one hand, she swung open the front door and barreled outside, crashing into Liz head-on. The force of her movement coupled with the weight of her suitcase sent her tiny roommate staggering backward off the step and onto the lawn.

"Where are you going?"

"Where have you been?"

Julia's query brought a flush to Liz's cheeks. She was still wearing her red dress from the night before, though it was looking much the worse for wear. A wine stain spotted the bodice and one strap hung limply off her shoulder. Her sling-back heels dangled from one hand. Her panty hose were nowhere in sight. Her hair was a mess and a slightly feverish glaze tinged her dark eyes.

"I've been, ah . . . out," she said, dodging Julia's gaze. "Out . . . to get some danishes." Her eyes hit on the bakery bag she held in her right hand and widened in surprise, as if she'd never seen it before. She held it up as evidence. "Danishes."

"You're a little overdressed for the bakery, aren't you?"

"I'm getting my money's worth out of this gown." She gave Julia's suitcase a pointed look and arched a brow. A warm smile bent the corners of her mouth upward. "I take it Storm convinced you. I knew he was the man of your destiny."

Julia frowned. This was exactly the conversation she had wanted to avoid having. "He convinced me he's a cad. San Diego is my destiny. I'm going on vacation."

Liz's eyes rounded like quarters. Her smile changed into an *O* of dismay. "But what happened? Last night when you both disappeared I thought everything was fine, I thought—"

"Last night was a long time ago. Things can change in a hurry."

"Tell me about it," Liz muttered almost to herself.

"I'd love to, but there's no time," Julia said. "My cab is here. Take a gander at the front page of the *Trib*. That says it all." She adjusted her grip on the handle of her suitcase and started down the walk toward the yellow cab waiting at the curb. "If S.T. calls, tell him I left him before he could leave me this time."

"But Julia—!"

Julia shoved her suitcase into the backseat of the car and climbed in. The cab was moving before Liz could make it to the sidewalk.

Grumbling in Spanish, Liz watched the taxi disappear around the corner, then turned and hurried back to the house. She dug the newspaper out of a potentilla shrub, took one glance at the headline, and groaned. Some days it just didn't pay to be a spy in the name of love. With that thought uppermost in her mind, she went inside to make a phone call.

S.T. stalked down the wide aisles of the Minneapolis airport, boot heels ringing dully against the floor, eyes narrowed and directed straight ahead of him. He passed more than one person who recognized him, but he was in no mood for autographs and that message was clearly telegraphed by the set of his jaw, the hard line of his mouth, the purposeful strides. He was a man on a mission. Crowds parted for him. Those fans who weren't due to depart on planes fell into step behind him, bright-eyed and curious.

He hadn't appreciated waking up alone. After the night he'd spent with Julia, he had been certain things were on the right track between them. The love that had shone in her eyes had been absolute, pure, strong, with nothing held in reserve. In the moments before they had finally drifted off to sleep, he had held her in his arms and felt whole, complete in a way he had never felt before, as if the final missing puzzle piece had at last slipped into place, filling up a hole in the big picture of his life. Waking up without her in his arms or even his bed had been an unpleasant surprise. To discover she wasn't even in the suite had scared the hell out of him.

His stomach clutched as he remembered turning around in the sitting room and having his gaze land squarely on the newspaper headline. Of all the rotten luck. He was angry that those negotiations had been leaked to the press, but that was nothing compared to the anger he felt when he thought that Julia hadn't even bothered to confront him about it. She had taken one look, assumed the worst, and bolted.

Well, if she thought she could just ditch him and fly off to California, she could think again. He had wooed and coaxed and fairly begged her to believe in him. The time had come for drastic measures. The time had come for action.

He spotted her standing in line, waiting to board her flight. Her eyes widened as she watched him vault over the railing in the waiting area. She turned to face him, armed with a shoulder bag that she held up in front of her like a shield. The people in line regarded her with wary suspicion and gave her a wide berth as they consulted their tickets, obviously hoping they wouldn't get stuck sitting next to this crazy woman.

"Stay back!" she ordered. "I mean it, S.T. Touch me and I'll scream."

"We'll see about that."

They squared off like a pair of wrestlers, each measuring the distance between them, calculating odds, planning strategy. S.T. stayed on the offensive, backing Julia out of line. She kept her eyes on him as she shuffled backward. A large crowd gathered to watch. S.T. could hear them laughing, but he tuned them out, his attention riveted on the woman before him, *his* woman, *his* soul mate, who was about to hop a plane out of his life.

"You're coming with me, Legs," he declared in a voice that brooked no disobedience.

Julia scowled at him. "You'll have to knock me out and hog-tie me first."

"Don't tempt me, baby," he warned, working his way left and forward, herding her toward a row of vinyl-covered chairs that were bolted to the floor. "I just might take you up on it."

"Yeah, you would," she sneered. "Where's your camera crew, Dalton? They can get some film of this to send to the network. You'd love the publicity, wouldn't you? Maybe they'll give you your own sit-com. *Taken by Storm*, the story of an obnoxious, double-dealing jerk and the idiot women who fall for him."

"Oh, you've got it all figured out, haven't you?" he snapped, his temper rising like mercury in a thermometer. "You've got my whole future planned out for me, don't you? Never mind that you haven't bothered to ask me about it. Never mind that you just count every word of love and commitment I've given you as a lie—"

"You wouldn't know commitment if it fell on your head with an anvil attached. 'All I want is you and the ranch and peace and quiet,'" she quoted in a mocking tone of voice that set S.T.'s teeth on edge. "There's the biggest crock of sh—"

"It's the truth, dammit!" he thundered as his pulse started pounding in his temple and a red haze drifted like mist before his eyes. "And if you won't stand here and listen, then, by God, I'll take you somewhere you damn well won't have any choice."

He took an aggressive step toward her. Julia retreated, the backs of her legs hitting the edge of a chair. She yelped as she lost her balance, flinging her arms wide. S.T. barreled forward, head down, and caught her in the midsection with his shoulder, sweeping her off her feet into the air in a fireman's lift that did nothing to enhance her dignity.

Julia screamed, arms and legs flailing. She clobbered him on the head with her purse, knocking his hat off. The shift of her weight sent him staggering sideways, but he caught his balance and wrapped both arms around her long legs to keep her from kicking the stuffing out of him.

"Lord, I'm gettin' too old for this," he groaned as he hefted her back into position with a shrug of his shoulder.

The crowd let out a roar, laughing and whooping and clapping their hands, shouting encouragement and suggestions. People had stopped boarding the plane to witness the ruckus, and every last one of them was on S.T.'s side. A chant of "Storm! Storm! Storm!" began building around them.

"This is disgusting," Julia said, panting for breath. "What ever happened to women's rights?"

"Overruled by the laws of nature, baby," S.T. drawled, flashing the crowd a wave and a grin. "You can't fight a storm."

"Yeah, well, we'll see what the laws of man have to say about it. Just wait until the security guards get here."

S.T. gave a bark of laughter. "Who do you think is leading all the cheers, sweetheart?"

He turned around to give her a view of two uniformed guards standing at the edge of the crowd, clapping and whistling. One raised a fist in the air and yelled, "Way to go, Storm!"

"Oh, great," Julia snarled. "Now you're corrupting the constabulary. You think you can get away with anything, don't you?"

"Oh, I don't know about that, honey," he said as he headed for the aisle. "But I'm gettin' away with you, and that's all I care about."

"And just where do you think you're taking me?"

"Montana."

"Oh, no. You can just forget that," she said, squirming frantically, her right knee hitting him in the diaphragm and making him grunt. "I'm sick of you thinking you can just toss me over your shoulder like a sack of feed and cart me off."

"No offense, honey, but you weigh a sight more than any sack of feed I ever carried," he said between his clenched teeth, hefting her up again and resettling her on his shoulder in a move that knocked an *oof* from her.

"Oh, thanks. You have a real way with women, Dalton," she snarled. "The Neanderthals could have taken lessons from you."

"That's not what you were saying last night, baby."

"Last night I was temporarily insane."

"Crazy about me."

"Crazy because of you is more like it."

They passed the ticket counters and crossed the main concourse, headed for the row of big glass doors that led to the parking facilities. People stared and pointed. Many called out to S.T. Some took pictures. No one tried to stop him. He had left his truck parked in a tow-away zone, but no one had attempted to move it. Bingo sat in the cab, leaning against the passenger door with his head hanging out the window, waiting patiently.

S.T. went around to the driver's side, opened the door, and stuffed Julia in. She thought about struggling again, kicking him in the head, and taking off with his truck, but she had no doubt she would be set upon by a mob of his fans. They would rush out into the street to form a human barricade, and that would be the end of her escape. With a fatalistic sigh, she swung her feet to the floor and arranged herself between her captor and his dog. Bingo turned to give her a look of grave disappointment as S.T. put the truck in gear and they started down the curving road that led away from the main terminal building.

"You shouldn't have run, Julia," S.T. said, his eyes on the traffic around them as they merged onto the highway and picked up speed.

Julia stared at his profile, the hurt swelling up in her chest all over again. "You shouldn't have lied to me."

"I never lied to you."

"Well, you sure as hell didn't tell me the truth!"

"I did too. I told you I want you and the ranch. That's it. That's the truth. I'm not interested in the network job."

"You're not interested in making two million dollars?" she said, incredulous.

He gave a snort as he pulled in behind a city bus with a hot-pink "Julia, Be Mine" sign on the back. "Hell, Legs, I've got more money than I know what to do with now. I don't need to go looking for a job."

"No," Julia said, eyes glued to S.T.'s grinning likeness on the sign. "The job came looking for you. All the fame and fans of football without having to get beat up every week. Travel, exposure—"

"I've had all the travel I can take. I want a home, a family," He turned his head and gave her a fiercely intense look, blue eyes burning like twin gas jets. "I want you."

Julia frowned, shoving aside the automatic response of her body to his predatory look and claim. "For how long? How long before you start missing the limelight, the fans, the fuss? How long am I going to hold your interest over that, S.T.?"

"Forever. Dammit, Julia, I thought we had this settled last night."

"I thought so too," she said sadly, thinking back to how happy she had felt lying in his arms, believing that she was going to give him her heart again and that it would not be broken a fourth time. "Then the newspaper came."

"Why didn't you come to me with it?" he demanded as he exited the highway.

"Why didn't you tell me abut the offer in the first place?" she countered.

"Because I knew you'd go off the deep end. I didn't see any need to go through all that, since I wasn't going to take the job anyway."

"Oh, that's brilliant logic!" Julia said with a sarcastic laugh. "What else aren't you bothering to tell me about? Maybe you've been asked to run for president? Maybe you've been named Mr. Nude Universe? Are you going to tell me now, or do I get to wait and read it on the front page of a tabloid while I'm standing in line at the supermarket?"

S.T. hissed a sigh through his teeth and said nothing. This didn't seem like the prudent moment to mention a new offer for product endorsements. She would likely try to bash his skull in with that bag of bricks she called a purse. Besides, that part of his life was over. What difference did it make how many offers he got? He wasn't taking any of them.

"I wanted you to trust me," he said as he slowed the truck and turned into a blacktop drive that led toward a row of long, dirt-brown structures.

Julia was too stunned by what he'd said to notice their surroundings. "You wanted me to trust you, so you lied to me?"

"I didn't lie."

"Sin of ommission, then. Same thing." She shook her head. "God, you're amazing. You think you can just bull your way back into my life and run things however you see fit, twist the truth around to suit you, manipulate my friends, drag me around like a rag doll."

She ran out of words as the truck rolled to a halt and she looked around for the first time, her brow furrowing as she took in the deserted stretches of tarmac. Above the nearest building was a bright-orange wind sock pointed north, looking like a giant fluorescent condom against the blue of the sky. Julia felt her stomach start a slow barrel roll. "Where are we?"

"An airport."

"I liked the other one better. They have my luggage."

S.T. gave her a wolf's smile. "Baby, you're not gonna need luggage where we're going." He lifted his devil's eyebrows in a look of mock innocence. "Trust me."

Ten

"I can't believe you're actually doing this," Julia said, her voice breathless with shock as S.T. fastened her seat belt across her lap and gave it a tightening tug. She looked up at him, her eyes round. "You're kidnapping me. You're kidnapping me and taking me to Montana."

"That's about it in a nutshell, sweetheart," he said, calm, unruffled, as if he did this sort of thing every day. Crouched over to keep from bumping his head, he wedged his way between the two front seats of the single-engine plane and sidled back to check on Bingo. The dog had been relegated to a roomy wire-mesh crate that was strapped securely to the floor behind the second set of seats, a position Bingo obviously felt well beneath his dignity. Julia watched as the German shepherd gave S.T. a scathing glare, then turned and lay with his back to his master.

"Yeah, well," S.T. grumbled, "you'll get over it. I'm only doing this for your own good."

"Are you talking to me or the dog?" Julia asked dryly.

"Both, I guess."

"I fail to see how dragging me to Montana is going to benefit me in any way."

S.T. grinned at her. "Sure it will."

He edged sideways between the seats again, giving Julia an up-close-and-personal view of his fly. She bit her lip and tried not to notice the way his faded jeans molded the bulge of his manhood, tried not to notice the instant rush of heat her hormones shot through her. He slid into his seat and glanced over at her.

"You don't believe all I want is you and the ranch. I'll show you different." His eyes crinkled at the corners and glittered with mischief. "I figure by the time we've had five or six babies you'll be ready to believe me."

Another gust of heat swept through Julia as a barrage of mental images assaulted her—S.T. making love to her, her belly rounding with their child, a dark-haired baby nursing at her breast. They were fantasies she had allowed herself to indulge in recently. Fantasies that had died a swift, cold death when she'd seen that newspaper. Now they rose from the ashes, even though her logical mind tried to forbid it.

S.T. leaned close. His breath was warm and minty against her cheek. "I can see it too, Julia," he murmured. His left hand cupped one breast, his thumb brushing her nipple to instant attention through her T-shirt. She shivered, hating herself for reacting to him this way when she had decided she couldn't trust him. "We'll make it happen, baby," he whispered, brushing his lips against the corner of her mouth. "All you have to do is believe."

"And if I click my heels three times, will I find myself back in Kansas?" she managed to ask, her sarcasm not quite coming through the trembling in her voice as her emotions went to war inside her.

He pulled back slowly, the look on his face a mix of speculation and hurt he quickly hid with a pair of mirrored aviator sunglasses. "Nope, but you're gonna find yourself in Montana, Dorothy, so you might as well sit back and enjoy the ride."

Julia doubted enjoyment was going to be any part of this ride. In the first place, she was determined to be miserable. Her heart had been broken, her dreams dashed, and the bastard who had caused it all was kidnapping her! She had every right to be angry. In the second place, she was none too keen on flying in anything that didn't carry a full complement of airline attendants. Growing up in the vast expanse of Montana ranch country, she had gone up many times in planes this size and smaller and had never overcome the feeling that she was hurtling through space inside a Ping-Pong ball. There was no reason to think this time would be any different. In fact, with S.T. at the controls it was probably going to be worse. She stifled a moan at the mental image of him grinning like a maniac and putting the plane through a series of stunt rolls.

The image faded as she watched him put on a headset and adjust switches and dials on the instrument panel. His concentration was absolute. The laidback, fun-loving cowboy demeanor had fallen aside again, revealing the determined man beneath. She looked for some hint of the boy she had known, of the younger man who had left her, but saw neither. Her heart picked up a beat as she studied the strong line of his beard-shadowed jaw, the faint creases beside his mouth and eyes, the deep furrow across his forehead as he studied the gauges and spoke in coded gibberish to the control tower. This was a man to be reckoned with.

They were both grown up, she reminded herself. Still, the past lingered around them like a shadow, drawing them together, holding them apart, manipulating them like puppets. Or was she the only one being manipulated? Was she allowing the past to control her, to color her judgment? She wanted to say no, but as the plane's engine fired and the craft began its noisy trip toward the runway, she found she couldn't.

In minutes they were airborne, the ground falling away beneath them as the plane climbed the sky with a roar. Julia took a deep breath and tried to control the acrobatics of her stomach by distracting herself, taking in all the rich appointments of the plane. This was no charter hired out on weekends by the local flying school. The seats were butter-soft gray leather; the trim on the instrument panel and doors looked like teak.

"Whose plane is this?" she asked, raising her voice to be heard above the engine.

"A friend's," S.T. said. He flashed her a Cheshire-cat smile. "Nice of him to loan it to me on such short notice, huh?"

"Oh, yeah," Julia said dryly, damning the man and his many friends. "He's a real prince."

They flew west and north, quickly leaving the sprawling metropolitan area behind them for the patchwork of farm fields and narrow ribbons of roads. Eventually S.T. pulled the headset down so it rested around his neck like a collar.

"You all right, honey?" he asked, reaching over with his right hand to rub Julia's shoulder. Her muscles were knotted with tension. Most of the color had gone out of her face as they had taken off. Guilt had begun to scratch at S.T.'s conscience a little. He knew she didn't like to fly. He knew she didn't like to be bullied. But dammit, he hadn't seen any other way of getting the message across.

She gave him a sulky look. "Yeah, I'm swell. I love being kidnapped and rocketed across the country in an overblown station wagon with wings."

"Would it help if I told you I love you?" he asked gently.

"It would help if you'd take me home."

"That's what I'm doing."

"You know I hated Montana," she said peevishly.

"You hated living with your aunt and uncle," S.T. clarified. "You hated being an outsider. You hated that your daddy was on the other side of the world. You never hated Montana. I remember the way you looked at the mountains, the way you'd lie in my arms and listen to the wind in the grass, the way your eyes lit up when we'd watch the elk come down to water. That's Montana—the sky, the mountains, the wildlife. You never hated that."

"I hated it when you left," Julia admitted in a small voice. She remembered too well what it had been like after he'd gone away to college. It had been even worse than her previous feelings of abandonment, because all the things she had found solace in were shrouded with memories of S.T., and S.T. had no longer been there to share them with her.

"I won't be leaving this time, sweetheart," he promised.

"I was ready to believe that last night. Now—"

"Now you're ready to believe something the newspaper couldn't even confirm," he said, his temper rearing. His brows snapped together in a fierce hawkish expression above the rugged bridge of his nose. "Why is that, Julia? Why are you willing to believe the worst of me? And don't give me that crap about my track record. You know damn well I'm not the same man who ran away from you before."

She looked at him, unable to see his eyes behind the mirrored lenses of his sunglasses but feeling the penetrating quality of his stare just the same. His jaw was set like a slab of granite. His intensity was almost frightening.

"You love me," he declared in a harsh voice, leaning across the narrow space between their seats. "Say it." He slid his fingers into her hair and gripped the back of her head. "Say it, Julia."

"I—I love you," she stammered, cursing herself as tears of frustration and fear and weakness rose in her eyes like dewdrops.

S.T.'s stone mask fell away and he stroked her with a hand that wasn't at all steady. "I'm sorry, baby," he whispered hoarsely. He pressed a kiss to her cheek. A tremor shuddered through his body as he realized the edge his desperation had driven him to. "I'm sorry I scared you. I just want so much for us to have a future together. I want so much for you to believe in me—in us."

Julia watched as he sat back, shoved his sunglasses up on top of his head, and pinched the bridge of his nose with a thumb and forefinger. He looked tired, stressed. He had obviously not taken time to shave before coming after her. By the look of his hair, he hadn't bothered to run more than his fingers through it. The shirt he had on was a favorite old chambray that was slightly rumpled from a previous wearing. He looked vulnerable, and Julia couldn't stop her heart from wanting to reach out to him.

"I want to believe in that too, S.T.," she said. "But if I do and it falls out from under me again . . . I don't think I could survive it." She looked out the window at the emptiness of the sky, rubbing her hands against the sudden chill on her bare arms. "You're asking me to leave everything—my friends, a job I love, the home I've made for myself—"

"Your safety net," he said. "The cocoon you've made to protect yourself from getting hurt."

"And what's wrong with that?" she demanded. "All things considered, I'd be pretty stupid not to protect myself, wouldn't I? Jeez, you make me sound like an emotional cripple."

"I didn't say that. But you've got to be willing to risk something for love. How else can you know if it's the real thing? If you've got all kinds of padding to fall back on, there's no risk, you're certain you won't get hurt. What kind of love is that?"

The safe kind, Julia thought. The kind most people were happy to settle for.

"Think about it. If you're willing to take my hand and go out on a limb with me with no safety net, no tie lines, and we make it, then we know what we've got together is strong and special. It's the difference between living and just existing, Julia. You can reach for the brass ring or you can settle for a handful of grass. I want us to reach for that ring together."

"I reached for it before and got a handful of air."

He gave her another of his determined looks, eyes narrowed, mouth grim. "I love you, Julia. I'd do anything to prove that, risk everything I have. Everything. What do you want me to do? Write in the sky for you? Go up and get you the moon? I'd give it to you on a silver platter if I thought it would make you believe me when I tell you all I want is you and the life we can make together."

The moment hung there, waiting for her to say something. But it ticked past and the window of opportunity slid closed. S.T. turned away from her, dropping his sunglasses back into place and pulling the headset on, shutting himself off from her. Julia shifted uncomfortably in her seat, acutely aware of the man beside her. He seemed suddenly caught up in the task of taking readings and making adjustments, talking to some unseen person in a language that sounded as foreign to Julia as Martian.

He would do anything for her. Buy billboards. Take out ads. Make a fool of himself. Wear his heart on his sleeve. Park a giant plastic cow in her yard. Kidnap her. But when it came right down to it, it wouldn't matter what he was willing to do. It wouldn't matter to what length he was willing to go. When it came right down to it, it was up to her. She could go out on that limb and take a chance on his love or cling to her safety.

Her troubled gaze drifted out the window. It was a long long way to the ground, literally and figuratively, and there was nothing to break the fall.

They set down on an unpaved private strip later that afternoon. Julia had no idea where they were, but it wasn't the part of Montana where they had grown up. The country around them was open and treeless, acres and acres of golden wheat waving in the summer wind. The landscape was broken only by a weathered old airplane hangar that might have been squatting there on the wheat plain for fifty years or more and a big old stark white farmhouse that had been there even longer.

"Place belongs to some friends of mine," S.T. said, setting his headphones aside and unbuckling his seat belt. "I told them we'd stay the night here and go on to the ranch tomorrow."

Julia made no comment. S.T. didn't wait for one, at any rate. He made his way to the back of the plane and let Bingo out of his crate. Julia watched out the window as the dog dashed up and down the landing strip, stretching his long legs, ears flat to his head, tongue streaming out the side of his mouth, ecstatic to be free.

A diminutive blond woman came out of the hangar wearing baggy jeans and a T-shirt the color of scrambled eggs. She shaded her eyes with one hand and waved a faded red rag in greeting, a sunny smile beaming across her features. Bingo made a beeline for her, nearly knocking her off her feet with his enthusiasm. A stocky man with a shock of curly brown hair emerged from the shadows of the hangar laughing, shooing the dog away with a ratty baseball cap. His face was a series of light and dark streaks— the whites of his eyes, a band of dirt, a flash of white teeth, a line of grease. Julia unfolded herself from her seat, gathered up the only bag she had—her purse— and left the plane, wondering what adventure was in store next.

S.T. introduced the couple as "Blockhead" and Marni Malone. Julia arched a brow at the first name. Marni chuckled.

"He wanted that on our marriage license," she said to Julia, her accent making it obvious she hailed from New York or New Jersey, someplace a long way from where they were standing. "I drew a great big fat line right there."

"Blockhead used to be my center," S.T. explained.

"Yeah, back in the Stone Age," the big man drawled. He clamped a greasy hand on S.T.'s shoulder and gave him a little shake. He started to offer his right hand to Julia, but Marni intercepted it with a grimace and held it up in front of his face so he could see the state of it. He gave a grunt and a shrug, green eyes twinkling in his dirty face as he looked at Julia. "You can call me Scottie, but I'll answer to most anything."

Marni rolled her eyes. "Especially 'dinner is served.'"

Julia found herself instantly liking the couple. They were warm and funny and obviously in love. Scottie proudly showed them around his hangar, which held two different small planes, one of which he had been working on—the engine was exposed and an array of tools lay on a tarp on the floor. He explained to Julia that he did a little teaching, a little mechanic work, a little crop dusting, a little shuttle service, a little stunt flying at local fairs and festivals.

"Jack-of-all-trades, master of none," Marni interjected with a wink and pinch to her husband's rock-solid belly.

"Master of you," he growled, taking a playful swat at her bottom.

She danced out of his reach, shaking a finger at him. "Hey, hey, hey! No manhandling pregnant lady!"

"You're expecting?" S.T. asked, his face lighting up with pleasure as he caught Marni in a hug. "That's great news, honey!"

"I'll say," she said dryly, a blush blooming on the apples of her cheeks. "It took us long enough."

"Yeah, well," S.T. drawled, rolling his eyes Scottie's way. "Look what you got to work with, sweetheart."

Scottie let out a bellow of mock outrage and the men fell into a shoving match, knocking each other around.

Marni shook her head and waved a hand at them. "Come on, Julia. We'll go inside and get dinner while they get primitive."

If Marni thought it odd that Julia had no luggage, she didn't mention it. She showed Julia to a sunny yellow bedroom on the second floor of the big house, and gave her a stack of fluffy towels and directions on getting sixty-year-old plumbing to cooperate. When Julia was done washing up, she found a freshly ironed blue work shirt laid out on the bed for her. *Scottie* was embroidered in red above the pocket. It was far too big for her, but it was clean and comfortable.

"Thanks for the loan," she said as she found Marni in the big kitchen chopping vegetables. "My luggage is probably on the beach in San Diego about now, sipping a margarita. Here, let me help with that."

Marni scooted over at the work island, sliding a knife and a pile of carrots in Julia's direction. They set to work together as if they'd been doing it for years.

"Storm tells us you're a nurse."

"Yeah. In an emergency room back in Minneapolis."

"That must be exciting. Me, I used to gag at the sight of blood, but I came out here to be with Scottie and I decided that had to change in a big hurry. There's no doctor around here for miles. First thing I did was take the EMT course."

"Where are you from?"

"The Bronx. I'm a long way from home, right?" She shook her head, then swiped her bangs back with her forearm, hardly breaking the rhythm of her work. "I was working in public relations for a big sporting goods outfit when I met Scottie. He was playing for the Giants then—well, sitting on their bench, anyway—and I fell like a rock. Then he ups and tells me he's been cut and he's moving to Montana to be a pilot." She rolled her eyes and gave a shout of laughter. "God, Montana! I half expected to be trampled by buffalo or eaten by a bear or something when I came here. I'd never been west of Newark in my life!"

"But you love it here," Julia said quietly.

"Hey, as long as I'm with my Scottie, I don't care if we live on the moon."

They chopped in silence for a minute, then Marni scooped up the vegetables and tossed them into a pot of water on the stove. Julia slid onto a stool at the counter and dangled her hands between her knees as she watched Marni and thought about herself and S.T.

Marni shot her an assessing sideways glance as she stirred a boiling pot of pasta. "Storm's making an example of us, right?" Her mouth quirked into a wry smile and she shook her head. "Men. They kill me. They think they're being so clever."

"So are you going to give me the Storm Dalton sales pitch?" Julia asked.

Marni gave an elaborate shrug. "What? Me? Hey, if you love him, you love him. I can't make that decision for you. Only your heart can know for sure." She turned down a burner and wiped her hands on a towel, then gave Julia a sheepish grin. "But he *is* a great guy."

The four of them spent much of the evening in the kitchen at the big trestle table eating and talking, S.T. and Scottie trying to outdo each other with wild stories about their playing days together. Eventually they retired to the living room where they watched home videos of Scottie doing stunt flying at fairs and pulling advertising banners across slices of blue sky.

At ten o'clock Marni, her body adjusting to the early stages of pregnancy, fell asleep leaning against her husband's beefy shoulder. Scottie bid Julia and S.T. a soft good night and carried his wife upstairs to their room.

S.T. watched them go, then turned to Julia with a

tender look that made her heart catch. "They're happy," he said simply.

Julia could have pointed out that Scottie and Marni were two completely different people in completely different circumstances, but she didn't. The fact that S.T. had brought her here meant too much. Of all his grand gestures, perhaps it meant the most because he was trying to tell her he could be happy with a simple life. A part of her wanted to grasp that idea and cling to it and a part of her was still clinging to that newspaper headline about a job of travel, glamour, and money. The nights in Montana were long and quiet. There was nothing glamorous about working a ranch.

They went up to their room in silence. Julia slipped her jeans off and laid them across a chair. She pulled the length of mangled nylon from her hair and set to work combing out the long tresses, staring into the mirror above the dresser. S.T. came to stand behind her, his shirt open, tails hanging out, the top button of his jeans undone.

"You still mad at me for kidnapping you?" he asked softly, his eyes on hers in the mirror.

"It *is* a federal offense," Julia reminded him with a wry look.

S.T. gave her a lopsided smile and shrugged his big shoulders. "A man's gotta do what a man's gotta do."

"The cowboy credo." Julia drew her comb slowly through another section of thick, long hair, her expression thoughtful. "I like your friends."

"I'm glad. The big question is, do you like me?"

"Some times more than others."

"Guess I'll just have to take what I can get and work on the rest." He lifted her hair aside and pressed a lingering kiss to the back of her neck. His hands came up beneath her arms and around her rib cage, sliding up to cup her breasts through the soft fabric of the old work shirt.

Julia let her head fall back against his shoulder

and savored the warm tingling that ribboned through her at his touch. Love and fear intertwined like vines inside her, squeezing her heart.

S.T. snuggled closer, pulling her bottom against the hard ridge of his arousal, the heel of one hand pressing low against her belly, against the emptiness inside her that suddenly ached to be filled. His breath came harder, stirring the tendrils of hair at the nape of her neck. The touch of his hand became more insistent on her breast.

Julia twisted out of his grasp and took a step away, head down, hair falling in a curtain against the left side of her face. "Not tonight, S.T.," she murmured. "I need to think."

S.T. frowned as he reached out and drew her back into his embrace. "No. You think too much," he murmured, his voice husky and low. He brushed a sprig of flame-colored hair back from her temple with gentle fingers. His gaze, deep and blue, caught hers and held it. "Tonight you need to feel. Just feel, Julia. How good it is between us. How much I love you." He pulled her hand up between them and pressed it flat against his chest as he had done the first day he'd come back into her life. "Feel my heart. It beats for you, baby," he whispered. "Only you. No one else, nothing else. Just you."

She looked up at him with wide eyes and S.T. lowered his mouth to hers before he could read the uncertainty there. Tonight he needed to feel too. He needed to feel Julia beneath him and around him, her silky warmth caressing him and welcoming him.

He felt as if he had clutched the last straw and it was slipping through his grasp. Kidnapping her had been the act of a desperate man, and tonight that desperation was lodged in his heart like a jagged rock. What if she just plain didn't love him enough? What if she chose safety over risk? He could go back with her to Minneapolis, give up the idea of ranching, but then he would never know if he had her complete trust, and he knew in his heart he had to have all of her. They couldn't settle for something less, when they could have everything.

He slid the work shirt from her shoulders and let it drop to the floor, then allowed her to do the same for him. In a few moments they were stretched out naked on the iron bed, their bodies moving in a courtship dance as old as time. As badly as he needed her, S.T. forced himself to go slowly, to cherish every part of her, love every part of her with his hands and his mouth. He savored the sweet taste of her woman's body, gloried in the soft, wild sounds she made as she arched her hips to offer herself fully. He took her to the brink of fulfillment and held her there until she called his name in a soft, broken whisper. Then he joined her, joined her body with his, joined her at the edge of ecstasy and beyond.

When it was over and he held her sleeping form in his arms, he thought of tomorrow and all the days to come, of the future that stretched before him like a long, dusty road. Julia had to stay with him. He had to convince her. She was the love of his life. They had belonged together from that day by the lake when he had ridden up on his horse and caught her crying.

He stared out the window at a huge moon that seemed close enough to touch. *I'd give it to you on a silver platter if it would make you believe in me. . . .* He would give her anything, everything he had, everything he was. But he couldn't give her back her trust in him. He could only try to win it back.

Winning. He had devoted much of his life to it. For a time victory had come easily, but he had learned to fight to win too. He would win this time because he had to. His heart was depending on it . . . and so was Julia's. He would win this battle for love, he declared silently as he pressed a kiss to Julia's hair. He would win it or die trying.

Eleven

Julia woke alone. She looked across the expanse of rumpled sheets where S.T. had lain beside her and rubbed her palm against the mattress. It was cold. The soft, gray velvet color of the sky outside the window told her it was early. She sat up slowly, piling the pillows behind her and dragging the sheet up around her shoulders.

She missed him. She missed having his big, hard body next to hers, hogging the bed. She missed having his hairy legs twined with her smooth ones, missed his face beside hers on the pillow. She had wanted to wake up snug and warm in his arms and have him make slow, sweet love to her. That was when everything was right. That was when she felt safest. When she was in S.T.'s embrace she felt certain what they had together would last forever and nothing would tear them apart. Sitting here in bed alone, she found it too easy to let the old fears creep in. She looked out the window and saw nothing but Montana sky and wheat fields and felt as if she were the only person left on earth.

What was she going to do? Follow her heart and risk everything or follow her head and go back home to Minneapolis? In a perfect world she wouldn't have to make a choice. She and S.T. were soul mates, meant for each other in every way. But there was no such thing as a perfect world or perfect people, only perfect dreams. She had dreamed of loving S. T. Dalton, of sharing a home and building a family with him. Did she dare take a chance on that dream coming true, when her biggest fear was of that dream dying yet again?

The drone of an airplane engine slowly broke in on Julia's thoughts. Distant at first, it filtered in only at the edges of her consciousness, like a fly buzzing in a far corner of the room. But it grew louder and more insistent, the plane finally swooping low over the house like a giant bird of prey. Grabbing her borrowed shirt from the foot of the bed, Julia scrambled out of bed and went to the window. Scottie's red stunt plane was banking up and to the north, turning around for another pass over the house.

"I'll kill them both with my bare hands," Marni said from the doorway. Julia turned and bit her lip as she took in her hostess's appearance. Marni had one hand clamped to the top of her head, the other resting gingerly on her stomach. Her eyes were narrowed, her lips pinched, her skin a pasty white.

"Morning sickness?" Julia ventured.

Marni groaned. "It's the pits. Let me be the first to tell you. Everything makes it worse. Moving makes it worse. Noise makes it worse. Airplanes going over my head at six o'clock in the morning make it worse. What are they doing out there, anyway? Reenacting Pearl Harbor?"

"I'm not sure," Julia said, glancing back out the window. The plane had disappeared from her line of sight, but the engine whined on. "I was just going to go out and see. Want to come?"

"You go," Marni said with a grimace. "I'll be out as soon as I'm done paying homage to the porcelain throne."

With that she turned and dashed down the hall.

Julia watched her go, feeling a stupid mix of sympathy and envy. Brother, the lengths Storm Dalton could drive a woman to. She was actually felling jealous of someone who was being violently ill at that moment. Shaking her head in amazement, she hurried to dress, pulling on her panties and stepping into jeans as the plane buzzed overhead. It had made another pass over the house and was moving straight away as she ran out onto the front lawn.

Scottie stood in the middle of the yard with his hands on his hips and a big grin on his square face. "Well, what do you think?"

"I think you and Mr. Dalton are prime targets for a double homicide right about now," Julia said dryly. "Marni is none too excited about the wake-up call."

Scottie's expression was one of almost comic distress as he looked up at the big house. "Shoot. We woke Marni? I thought she'd sleep through it."

Julia rolled her eyes as she hugged herself against the early morning chill. "Yeah, go figure. The plane's only as loud as a buzz saw amplified about nine hundred times. What's he doing up there anyway?"

Another big grin broke across Scottie's face, and he thrust an arm toward the heavens. "Proposing!"

Julia's jaw dropped as she looked up at the sky. Trailing behind the little red plane was a length of mesh netting to which big red block letters had been fastened, spelling out "JULIA BE MINE."

"Aw, isn't that romantic?" Marni said, pulling an old varsity sweater around herself as she joined them on the lawn. She tilted her head back and looked up at the plane as it circled. The color instantly drained from her face. She turned to Julia with a pained smile. "Gee, that's sweet. Excuse me while I go throw up."

Scottie went back to the house with her, fussing around her like a giant mother hen every step of the way. Julia glanced from the couple up to the sky, warm ribbons unfurling inside her as she watched S.T. guide the plane in a graceful turn.

It *was* sweet and romantic, and slightly crazy. One more grand gesture to try to win her over. How was she supposed to resist a man who would write his love for her across the sky in a place where almost no one else would see? He wasn't doing this to impress a bevy of reporters. He wasn't doing it to impress Scottie or Marni. He was doing it for her.

Everything I do, I do for you, baby.

He brought the plane straight past her, flying low, and waved to her as he went by, giving her a big cat-that-got-the-canary grin. Julia waved him on, trying to make a face at him, but not able to repress her smile. He waggled the wings of the plane to let her know he'd seen her, then took it up into another big sweeping turn.

I love you, Julia. I'd do anything to prove that, risk everything I have.

All she really had to risk was her heart. She could get another job, make new friends, live anywhere. But she would never find another man who touched her soul the way this one did. They had belonged together all along. All she had to do was be willing to reach for that brass ring with him one more time.

He was bringing the plane back, flying no more than fifty feet above the ground as he passed the hangar. With one quick movement the plane rolled belly up and passed by the house upside down. Julia's heart vaulted into her throat. She felt every red blood cell she possessed turn ash gray.

"So what are you gonna say?" Scottie asked shyly as he came to stand beside her once again.

"Before or after I wring his neck for scaring me to death?" she asked, trying to mask the shaking in her voice with sarcasm.

Scottie waved her worries away. "That's nothing. Storm's a top-notch pilot. Shoot, he taught *me* that trick."

Julia didn't care. She held her breath until S.T. had turned the plane upright again, suddenly angry with him for doing something so foolish just to get her attention. Why couldn't he have proposed like any normal man over a quiet dinner in a nice restaurant?

Because then he wouldn't have been S.T. Because he saw risk as a way of proving his love. Because he loved infuriating her. He would probably still be doing it when they were old and toothless, raising her blood pressure to dangerous levels until the nursing home people threatened to put them in opposite wings of the building.

She shook her head, a wry smile canting one corner of her mouth as she watched the red plane climb and bank once again. The sun was breaking over the eastern horizon, turning the Montana sky fabulous shades of pink and orange above the unending fields of wheat. Julia snagged back a handful of wind-tossed hair and shaded her eyes with her other hand as she watched the plane move in a graceful arch.

"I'm going to say yes!" she shouted, her heart soaring upward with the plane as she let go of her safety line and committed herself to joining S.T. on his high wire.

And then the engine sputtered and died.

It took a second for Julia to realize something was wrong. Then the absence of sound hit her ears as if she had been suddenly rendered deaf. She took a step ahead feeling vaguely bewildered. The plane's engine gave one last shudder, and Julia breathed with it, relief flooding through her in a rush that ended just as abruptly, leaving dizziness swirling in its wake as a plume of black smoke billowed from the plane's nose.

"No," she murmured, stumbling forward. "No. No. *No!*"

She ran, legs pumping, body hurtling forward, mind feeling detached from it, as if they were two

completely individual entities. Her gaze held fast on
the plane that was falling out of the sky in slow
motion. Time became strangely elastic and Julia
thought for a moment that she might actually get to
the spot before the plane hit the ground, but that
wasn't what happened. She didn't hear the crash,
only the roar of her heart in her ears, but she
witnessed every detail—the right wing tip dipping
below the heads of wheat, the wing crumpling like a
piece of cardboard, the nose hitting immediately
after, the fuselage cartwheeling once, then going still,
smoke and dust rising from the wreckage, backlit by
the new dawn.

Julia plunged toward it, arms swimming through
the wheat stems. Scottie caught her from behind and
flung her backward, giving himself a lead on her. He
was tearing at the door of the plane by the time she
got to the wreck. He didn't glance at her, but kept to
his task, swearing a blue streak the entire time,
chanting curse words like a mantra as the sickening
smell of gasoline, hot metal, and scorched wheat
polluted the air. Julia stood back and watched him
work, only dimly aware that she was sobbing. Then
the door was open and Scottie was dragging S.T.
toward her as tongues of orange flame licked up
behind them.

In all her years as a trauma nurse Julia had never
been in the position of sitting in the waiting lounge
of an emergency room doing nothing. It seemed
completely unnatural. She should be down the hall
helping. She wished she could. Work focused her
brain, shut down emotions. There was a logic and
orderliness to nursing. There was no logic in the
waiting room, only fear and guilt.

*I love you, Julia. I'd do anything to prove that,
risk everything I have. Everything . . . I love you,*

Julia. What do you want me to do, write it in the sky for you?

She closed her eyes in pain as S.T.'s words came to her yet again and she was immediately confronted by the image of his face, the hurt in his blue eyes, the stubborn set of his jaw as he'd stared at her across the cockpit of the plane. She would have given anything to go back to that moment. Time had hung suspended between them, waiting for her to say something. All she had to do was tell him she loved him and that she was willing to take a chance on that love. But she had let that moment slide past. Clinging to her own fears, she had missed the chance, and S.T. had felt compelled to go on proving himself to her. Now he was in a hospital fighting for his life. And all she could do was sit and wring her hands.

Hands that were covered with S.T.'s blood. She had felt an initial blast of terror and panic at his condition when Scottie had dragged him from the plane, but she had shoved both aside and worked feverishly to stem bleeding and prevent shock and provide whatever other care she could. Marni had helped, her EMT training rising above her morning sickness. Scottie had radioed for the rescue helicopter from the nearest hospital and the chopper staff had allowed Julia to ride with them to the hospital. The whole thing—the accident, the wait for the helicopter, the flight to the hospital—had taken maybe an hour, an hour and a half. It seemed like days. And every minute they had to wait for the doctor's report seemed like an extra day to relive the guilt, an extra day to regret.

She had always loved him. That was the only thing that really mattered. Why couldn't she have seen that sooner? They had wasted enough time running away from each other and the love that had bound their hearts together all those years ago. Life was too uncertain to demand guarantees or wait for ideal conditions. What she had with S.T. was so rare. Many people searched their whole lives without finding that kind of love. She'd had it in her grasp and let it slip through her fingers because she'd been too afraid of losing it to hang on.

"He'll be okay," Marni murmured, pressing a cup of coffee into Julia's hand. She clutched her own cup and sat down in a boxy chair upholstered in the same color as the gray carpet on the floor.

"He'll be all right," Scottie mumbled, pacing restlessly back and forth across the width of the waiting room.

Julia watched him move. He was talking more to himself than anyone, trying to convince himself. Personally, she was beyond pep talks and had started making promises. If S.T. pulled through she would tell him she loved him every day, she would marry him, go anywhere with him, give him enough children to start his own football team.

The doors to the emergency room swung back and a stone-faced man in surgical green stepped out, pulling his cap off and running a hand through straight ink-black hair. There was a definite air of weariness about him, but authority still shone through in the light of his dark eyes and the set of his wide shoulders. Julia was on her feet instantly, moving toward him.

"You're Julia?" he asked. His handshake could have cracked walnuts. "I'm Dr. Eagle."

Julia said nothing. She merely stared into that carved-from-granite face and waited. He nodded almost imperceptibly. Something in his gaze calmed her and she felt tension drain from her muscles.

"Your Mr. Dalton is a lucky man," he said quietly. "Thanks to you, I'm told." He gave her a crooked smile that did much to humanize his stern countenance. "Marry him and stay in Montana, Miss McCarver. We need trauma nurses like you."

Julia skipped over the compliment and the job offer. "Can I see him?"

"For a minute."

Lying quietly on a bed in the recovery room, S.T. looked as if he'd been in a fight with a grizzly bear and lost. There were bruises and scratches on his face. His right leg was in a cast. He wore a pristine white-gauze bandage like a headband. The monitors beside the bed had been commonplace things to Julia, but now, when someone she loved was hooked up to them, they looked strange and forbidding. She locked her gaze on S.T.'s battered face and took his left hand in hers, her thumb rubbing against the cheap silver ring on his pinky. He opened one eye and focused it carefully on her face.

"Hi," she whispered, tears of mingled joy and relief and guilt and fear clogging her throat and brimming over her lashes. "You're a sight for sore eyes, cowboy."

"Probably a sight to make sore eyes," he mumbled, his voice dry and hoarse, thin as a ghost. "I blew it again, didn't I, Legs?"

Julia shook her head, impatiently snagging back a length of hair that had fallen across her cheek. "No. I blew it this time. I'll make it up to you, though. I promise."

"Cross your heart?" he asked, one corner of his mouth tugging up in a shadow of his famous grin.

Julia leaned over him and traced an X across his sternum. "You're my heart," she whispered, brushing her lips against his cheek. "I love you."

She wanted to hear the words from his lips as well, reassuring her, absolving her, but when she pulled back his eyes were closed and he had drifted back into a drug-induced sleep.

Dr. Eagle put a hand on her shoulder and gently drew her back from the bed. "You can tell him later."

"I will," Julia said resolutely, her mind already racing ahead to form the plan. "You bet I will."

S.T. cracked an eye open and peered through the slit in search of Nurse Sprocket, "The Iron Bun." The dour-faced matron and her giant hypodermic side-kick were nowhere to be seen. His room was empty, dark, and cool, the blinds drawn against the glare of morning sunshine. There was no sign of Julia, either. He had a vague memory of her bending over him with tears in her eyes, but he wasn't certain if it was real or imagined, and he had no idea when he might have seen her. Time had become completely distorted, stretching and constricting at random so that he had no idea if minutes had passed or hours or days. He knew he had been drifting in and out of sleep for some time, his mind wandering through dreams and blackness and snatches of reality that seemed almost as surreal as the dreams.

He was fully conscious now and a sense of urgency seized him. Julia. He had to see her. He had the terrible feeling that his latest stunt might have driven her away for good. Him and his blasted grand gestures. This one had nearly gotten him killed. That was going to score all kinds of points with Julia, who had already been afraid of being left behind. He was going to be damned lucky if she hadn't already climbed on a plane for Minneapolis.

He took stock of his injuries as he tried to sit up. Broken leg, broken ribs, minor concussion. Nothing he hadn't endured before; he just hadn't endured them all simultaneously. Damn, he thought as he eased himself back against the pillows, feeling as weak as a kitten, this was going to make chasing a lady complicated business.

The door to his room swung open and he jerked his head toward it, instantly regretting the move. Not only did it set off a bongo symphony inside his skull, it also sank his heart as his gaze landed on Scottie's bulky form. His friend offered an apologetic smile.

"I know I'm not nearly as pretty as Julia, but I did bring fudge."

"Did you bring the keys to this prison? I gotta get out of here, partner."

"You want me to break you out? Are you kidding?" Scottie cast a nervous glance over his shoulder at the door. "There's a nurse out there who looks like she could knock Refrigerator Perry on his butt."

S.T. scowled, restlessness stirring inside him. "I've got to see Julia."

"Is that all?" Scottie said, raising his brows toward the fringe of curly brown hair that framed his forehead. "Well, shoot, why didn't you say so? I can fix that."

Setting his container of fudge on the bedside table, he ambled around the foot of the bed to the window and slowly raised the blinds. S.T. watched him with a wary impatience. Outside, a patch of emerald lawn quickly gave way to asphalt parking lot, and at the edge of the lot the morning sun shone down on a small crowd of people gathered around the wheels of a long flatbed trailer. On the trailer stood a sign about the size of a billboard with a blowup of the photograph from the infamous Sunday-morning *Star Tribune* article—himself in a tux, Julia in her gown, smiling into his eyes as they danced. Beside the picture was one word printed in ten-foot-tall black letters: YES!

"I figured it was my turn for a grand gesture," Julia said as she stepped into the room.

S.T. turned slowly and feasted his eyes on her, hardly noticing as Scottie slipped out the door behind her. Her ragged old jeans hugged her long legs down to a pair of battered boots. The purple T-shirt she was wearing was new, with silhouettes of coyotes howling at a crescent moon. Her hair was in its usual state of disarray. These things he noticed only in the most abstract way, details to be catalogued and remembered later. His gaze homed in on her face, her large, soft doe eyes that were regarding him with a tender mix of love and longing. The look set his heart pounding with renewed hope. Maybe he hadn't blown it, after all.

"Come here," he commanded, holding his left hand out to her. She obeyed, twining her fingers with his as she came to sit on the edge of the bed. "Does that sign mean what I think it means?"

"Brother, they really are lax about educating athletes in the schools," Julia said, rolling her eyes. "Last I heard, yes meant one thing—yes."

S.T. knew she was expecting a snappy comeback, but he was too nervous to oblige. He had thought he'd lost her; now she was standing here telling him something he'd been almost literally dying to hear. He wondered dimly if he was hallucinating. He blinked hard, steeling himself as he waited for Julia's image to metamorphose into the frightening countenance of Nurse Sprocket. It didn't happen.

"You'll be mine?" he said softly, his gaze searching deep, past her eyes to her heart.

"I always was. I always will be," she whispered. "Forever and ever, amen."

A lone tear teetered at the edge of her lashes, then spilled over, and all the fear and anguish she'd felt the moment she'd realized his plane was going down rushed to the surface once again. "I was so afraid of losing you, *really* losing you."

"Aw, shucks," he said, squeezing her hand. "A little plane crash? You can't get rid of me that easy, baby."

"I could have lost you in the blink of an eye," Julia said soberly. "Things fell into perspective pretty fast when I saw that plane go down. I thought I'd been afraid before. I didn't know what fear was until I had to face the fact that you might be dead."

"I wasn't too pleased with the prospect myself," S.T. said dryly. "The last thing a man wants to do in the middle of a marriage proposal is crash and burn."

Julia's eyes flashed with a surge of temper at the reminder of the foolish risk he'd taken. "You could have just asked me with two feet on the ground, you know, you boneheaded, dirt-for-brains cowboy."

"How about flat on my back?" he asked, arching a brow.

"Try me," she challenged.

S.T. nodded slowly, working to keep a poker face as excitement began to bubble like champagne inside him. "Okay. Will you marry me, Julia? Will you come be a rancher's wife and raise a rancher's kids out in the middle of nowhere?"

Julia gave him a long steady look. "I will, if you're the rancher."

"No more fears about me leaving you for something better?"

She shook her head, eyes still on his. "There's nothing better than what we've got between us. I plan to remind you of that every day for the rest of our lives."

S.T. flashed her his famous grin, the devilish effect somewhat softened by the sheen of moisture in his eyes. "Is that a promise, Legs?"

Julia smiled at him tenderly and lifted his hand to trace an *X* on his chest. "Cross my heart."

Epilogue

The sky was a shade of blue that belonged on the inside of a china teacup, delicate and beautiful. Julia lay on her back in the grass, breathing deeply the scents of wildflowers and warm earth, listening to the soft lapping of the lake against the shore. It was a perfect way to spend a perfect day in a perfect place. All was right with the world—or it would be as soon as S.T. joined her.

The thought had no sooner crossed her mind than she heard the sound of hoofbeats. She raised up on her elbows and watched as he rode up the hill at a lazy canter. He sat on the big gray gelding with the ease of a man born to the saddle, shoulders back, head high. She could feel his laser-blue gaze on her long before she could see his eyes beneath the brim of his black Stetson. It brought a glow to the fire that stayed lit inside her these days.

She sat up and drew her long legs gracefully beneath her as he halted the horse before her with little more than a subtle shift of his weight.

"What are you doing down there?" he drawled.

"Whatever I please," she sassed back, a lazy smile pulling at her lips.

He tipped his hat back and leaned across the

pommel of his saddle, a Cheshire-cat grin curling the corners of his mouth. "How about pleasing me?"

Julia arched a brow at him. "I promised to have and to hold, didn't I?"

"Yep."

He swung down off the gelding and sent it off to graze, never taking his eyes off Julia. He walked toward her, still limping slightly but otherwise showing no sign of the accident that had nearly claimed his life. It still made Julia shudder to think that she had nearly lost him forever, not to a flashy career but to death. He was her soul mate, her heart. She didn't want to imagine life without him.

"Come here, cowboy," she said, rising and holding her arms open for him. "Now that I have you, I want to hold you all the time."

"Sounds good to me, Mrs. Dalton," S.T. murmured, hugging her close. She was his love, his life, his future. She always had been. Even though she'd been Mrs. S.T. Dalton for only a few weeks, he couldn't imagine his life without her in it, couldn't imagine falling asleep without her in his arms or waking up without her cuddled beside him. He brushed a kiss to her temple and lifted a hand toward the top button on the chambray work shirt she'd swiped out of his closet and was wearing.

"Not so fast, slick," she said dryly, pulling back just enough to reach into the breast pocket of his shirt. "What's this?"

"Oh, that." He chuckled as he glanced at the postcard that pictured an erupting Hawaiian volcano. "Just a note from the newlyweds."

Flipping the card over, Julia read aloud. "'Turns out he's not so boring after all! Love and happiness to you and the man of your destiny. *Mrs.* Robert Christianson. P.S. The New Traditionalism beats the old Me Decade hands down.'"

Julia couldn't help but chuckle. Liz and Robert married. Fire and ice. Impulsive, impetuous Liz and practical, pragmatic Robert. She never would have believed it if she hadn't seen it for herself.

"Well, how do you like that?" she said with a smile.

"I like it fine," S.T. drawled, reaching once again for the top button of her shirt. His gaze heated and his voice went low and rough. "How do *you* like it, Mrs. Dalton?"

Julia's body responded instantly to his signals, heat rippling through her like fluttering ribbons. She shot him a wicked look from under her lashes as the postcard dropped from her fingers. She slid her arms up around his neck and slowly pulled him down onto the grass.

"How do I like it?" she echoed, gazing up into the face of her husband, her eyes dark and warm with love and sparkling with mischief. "I like to be taken by storm."

S.T. grinned as he tossed his hat aside. "Well, ain't this my lucky day. . . ."

THE EDITOR'S CORNER

The coming month brings to mind lions and lambs—not only in terms of the weather but also in terms of our six delightful LOVESWEPTs. In these books you'll find fierce and feisty, warm and gentle characters who add up to a rich and exciting array of folks whose stories of falling in love are enthralling.

Let Joan Elliott Pickart enchant you with her special brand of **NIGHT MAGIC**, LOVESWEPT #534. Tony Murretti knows exactly what he wants when he hires Mercy Sloan to design the grounds of his new home, but he never expected what he gets—a spellbinding redhead who makes him lose control! Tony vowed long ago never to marry, but the wildfire Mercy sparks in his soul soon has him thinking of settling down forever. This book is too good to resist.

Fairy tales can come true, as Jordon Winters learns in award-winning Marcia Evanick's **GRETCHEN AND THE BIG BAD WOLF**, LOVESWEPT #535—but only after he's caught in a snowdrift and gets rescued by what looks like a snow angel in a horse-drawn sleigh. Gretchen Horst is a seductive fantasy made gloriously real . . . until he discovers she's the mayor of the quaint nearby town and is fiercely opposed to his company's plan to build new homes there. Rest assured that there's a happy ending to this delightful romance.

Terry Lawrence's **FOR LOVERS ONLY**, LOVESWEPT #536, will set your senses ablaze. Dave King certainly feels on fire the first time he kisses his sister-in-law Gwen Stickert, but she has always treated him like a friend. When they're called to mediate a family fight at a romantic mountain cottage, Dave decides it's time to raise the stakes—to flirt, tease, and tantalize Gwen until she pleads for his touch. You're sure to find this romance as breathlessly exciting as we do.

Janet Evanovich returns with another one of her highly original and very funny love stories, **NAUGHTY NEIGH-**

BOR, LOVESWEPT #537, for which she created the most unlikely couple for her hero and heroine. Pete Streeter is a handsome hellraiser in tight-fitting jeans while Louisa Brannigan is a congressman's aide who likes to play it safe. When these two get entangled in a search for a missing pig, the result is an unbeatable combination of hilarious escapades and steamy romance. Don't miss this fabulous story!

You'll need a box of tissues when you read Peggy Webb's emotionally powerful **TOUCHED BY ANGELS, LOVESWEPT #538**. Jake Townsend doesn't think he'll ever find happiness again—until the day he saves a little girl and she and her mother, Sarah Love, enter his life. Sarah makes him want to believe in second chances, but can her sweet spirit cleanse away the darkness that shadows his soul? Your heart will be touched by this story, which is sure to be a keeper. Bravo, Peggy!

Spice up your reading with **A TASTE OF TEMPTATION** by Lori Copeland, LOVESWEPT #539, and a hero who's Hollywood handsome with a playboy's reputation to match. Taylor McQuaid is the type that Annie Malone has learned only too well never to trust, but she's stuck with being his partner in cooking class. And she soon discovers he'll try anything—in and out of the kitchen—to convince her he's no unreliable hotshot but his own man. An absolutely terrific romance.

On sale this month from FANFARE are four fabulous novels. National bestseller **TEXAS! SAGE** by Sandra Brown is now available in the paperback edition. You won't want to miss this final book in the sizzling TEXAS! trilogy, in which Lucky and Chase's younger sister Sage meets her match in a lean, blue-eyed charmer. Immensely talented Rosanne Bittner creates an unforgettable heroine in **SONG OF THE WOLF**. Young, proud, and beautiful, Medicine Wolf possesses extraordinary healing powers and a unique sensitivity that leads her on an odyssey into a primeval world of wildness, mystery, and passion. A compelling novel by critically acclaimed Diana Silber, **LATE NIGHT DANCING** follows the lives of three friends—sophisticated Los Angeles women who are busy, successful, and on the fast track of romance and sex, because, like women everywhere, they hunger for a man to love. Finally, the ever-popular Virginia Lynn lets her imagination soar across the ocean to England in the historical romance **SUMMER'S KNIGHT**. Heiress Summer St. Clair is stranded penniless on the streets of London, but her terrifying ordeal soon turns to passionate adventure when she catches the glittering eyes of the daring Highland rogue Jamie Cameron.

Also on sale this month in the Doubleday hardcover edition (and in paperback from FANFARE in May) is **LADY HELLFIRE** by Suzanne Robinson, a lush, dramatic, and poignant historical romance. Alexis de Granville, Marquess of Richfield, is a cold-blooded rogue whose dark secrets have hardened his heart to love—until he melts at the fiery touch of Kate Grey's sensual embrace. Still, he believes himself tainted by his tragic—and possibly violent—past and resists her sweet temptation. Tormented by unfulfilled desires, Alexis and Kate must face a shadowy evil before they can surrender to the deepest pleasures of love. . . .

Happy reading!

With warmest wishes,

Nita Taublib

Nita Taublib
Associate Publisher/LOVESWEPT
Publishing Associate/FANFARE

*As wild and mysterious as the Louisiana swamp he called
home, Lucky Doucet was an infuriatingly attractive
Cajun no woman could handle. His solitary life left no
room for the likes of elegant Serena Sheridan, but Lucky
couldn't deny her desperate need to find her missing
grandfather. Serena felt unnerved, aroused, and excited
by the ruggedly sexy renegade, and as they traveled deeper
and deeper into the steamy Bayou Noir, Serena found she
couldn't resist the rebel whose gaze burned her with its
heat. . . .*

*In the following excerpt, Serena and Lucky meet for the
first time.*

CHAPTER ONE

"You want to do what, *chère*?"

Serena Sheridan took a deep breath and tried again. "I need to hire a guide to take me into the swamp."

Old Lawrence Gauthier laughed as if at the punch line of some grand joke. His voice rang out through the shop, drowning out the Cajun music coming from the radio on the cluttered shelf behind him as well as the noises of the all-star professional wrestling emanating from the black-and-white television that sat on the counter. Lawrence sat on a stool behind the counter, his slender legs crossed at the knees, slouching in a posture reminiscent of an egret on a perch— thin shoulders hunched, head low between them. His face was narrow, with a prominent nose and eyes like jet beads. His skin was tanned dark and lined like old leather.

His laughter ended in a fit of coughing. He reached for his cigarette makings and shook his head. "What for you wanna do dat, *chère*? You goin' after dem crawfish, you?" He laughed again, trying to shake his head and lick the edge of his cigarette paper at the same time.

Serena smoothed her hands down the front of the immaculate oyster-colored linen blazer she wore over a matching pencil-slim skirt. She supposed she hardly looked dressed to walk into such a place, much less make the request she had. "No, I'm not interested in fishing."

She looked around the store, hoping to spot someone else who might be able to help her. It was the middle of the day and Lawrence appeared to be the only person tending the dingy, dimly lit sporting goods store, though some banging noises were coming from behind him, from a room Serena knew to be an even dingier workshop where men fussed with their boats, drank beer, swapped outrageous tales, and passed around girlie magazines.

She knew because she had once snuck in there as a girl. A headstrong child, she had taken exception to being denied the chance to go in with her grandfather and had stowed away inside his bass boat under a canvas tarp. Her vocabulary had gained a number of choice words that day that their house-keeper had later attempted to wash out of her mouth with soap.

"I need to find my grandfather, Mr. Gauthier," she said. "Apparently he's gone out to his fish camp. I need someone to take me to him."

Lawrence looked at her, narrowing his eyes. Finally he shook a gnarled finger at her. "Hey, you dat Sheridan girl what left to be a doctor, no?"

"Yes."

"Yeah, yeah! *Mais yeah!*" He chuckled, tickled with his powers of recollection. "You lookin' for Big Giff."

"Yes, but I need someone to take me. I need a guide."

He shook his head, still smiling at her as if she were a dear but infinitely dimwitted child. "*Non, chérie,* all what fishin' guides we got 'round here is gone busy now til Monday. Lotta sports coming down to fish these days. 'Sides, ain't nobody crazy 'nough go out to Giff's. Go out there, get their head shot off, them!"

He sucked on his little cigarette, holding it between thumb and forefinger in an unconsciously European fashion. Half of it was gone before he exhaled. He reached out with his free hand and patted Serena's cheek. "Ah, *ma jolie fille,* ain't nobody crazy 'nough to go out to Big Giff's."

As he said it, a loud bang sounded in the shop behind him, followed by a virulent French oath. Lawrence went still with his hand halfway to a tin ashtray on the counter, an unholy light coming into his eyes, a little smile tugging at a corner of his mouth. "Well, mebbe there's somebody. Jes' how bad you wanna go, *chère?*"

Serena swallowed the knot of apprehension in her throat, clasping her hands together in front of her like a schoolgirl. Now was not the time for a faint heart. "It's imperative. I have to go."

He bent his head a little to one side and gave a Gallic shrug, then shouted over his shoulder. "Étienne! *Viens ici!*"

What Serena had braced herself for she wasn't sure, but it certainly wasn't the man who filled the doorway. The impact of his sudden presence had the effect of being hit with the shock wave of an explosion, jolting her chest with a hollow thud and literally making her knees go weak—a phenomenon she had heretofore not believed in.

Her first impression was of raw power. Broad shoulders, bulging biceps. His chest, bare and gleaming with a sheen of sweat, was massive, wide and thick, slabs of hard muscle beneath taut, tanned skin. The strong V of his torso narrowed to a slender waist, a stomach corrugated with muscle and dusted with black hair that disappeared beneath the low-riding waistband of faded green fatigue pants. Serena was certain she could live to be a hundred and never find a more prime example of the male animal.

She raised her eyes to his face and felt a strange shiver pass over her from head to toe, making her scalp tighten and her fingers tingle. He stared at her from under sleepy lids with large, unblinking amber eyes, eyes like a panther's. His brow was heavy and straight, his nose bold and slightly aquiline. His mouth did the most damage to her nervous system, however. It was wide, with lips so masterfully carved, so incredibly sensuous, they would have looked perfect on a high-priced call girl. The effect of that mouth on a face so masculine—all lean planes and hard angles and five-o'clock shadow—was blatantly sexual.

He regarded her with a subtle disdain that suggested he didn't much care for women other than to bed them— something he appeared to be capable of doing on a more than regular basis. Pulling a cigarette from behind his ear, he planted it in the corner of his mouth, lit it, and said something to Lawrence Gauthier in rapid Cajun French, a patois no Parisian could begin to understand. The dialect had nearly been eradicated by the Louisiana school system decades before. And although it was making a comeback of sorts due to the latest craze for all things Cajun, it was still not widely spoken. This man spoke it as if it were his primary language.

Having grown up in Louisiana's French Triangle, Serena had picked up the odd word and phrase, but he spoke too quickly for her to understand anything more than the implication. That was clear enough by Gauthier's reaction—another laughing and coughing fit and a slap on the shoulder for his barbarian friend.

Serena felt her cheeks heat with embarrassment as the man sauntered to the end of the counter and leaned a hip against it, all the while assessing her blatantly with those lazy amber eyes. She could feel his gaze like a tangible caress, drifting insolently over her breasts, the curve of her waist, the flare of her hip, the long length of her legs. She had never imagined it possible to feel so naked while dressed in a business suit.

He took a leisurely drag on his cigarette, exhaled, and delivered another line to keep Gauthier in stitches. Serena gave him her coolest glare, defending herself with hauteur. "Excuse me, but I was raised to believe it is extremely rude to carry on conversations not all those around you can understand."

One black brow sketched upward sardonically and the corner of that remarkable mouth curled ever so slightly. He looked like her idea of the devil on steroids. When he spoke to her his tone was a low, throaty purr that stroked her senses like velvet. "I told him you don' look like you're sellin' it or givin' it away," he said, the words rolling out of his mouth with an accent as rich as Cajun gumbo. "So what could I possibly want with you? I have no interest in *américaine ladies*."

He drawled the last word with stinging contempt. Serena tugged at the lapels of her blazer, straightening the uniform of her station. Her chin went up another notch above the prim collar of her fuchsia silk blouse. "I can assure you I have no *interest* in you either."

He pushed himself away from the counter and moved toward her with the arrogant grace of a born athlete. Serena stubbornly stood her ground as he stepped near enough for her to feel the heat of his big body. Her heart fluttered in her throat as he stared down at her and raised a hand to smooth it back over her hair.

"That's not what your eyes are tellin' me, *chère catin.*"

Serena dragged in a ragged breath and held it, feeling as if she were going to explode from sheer fury. She slapped his hand away and took a step back from him. "I didn't come here to be insulted or manhandled. I came here to hire a guide, Mister—"

"Doucet," he supplied. "Étienne Doucet. Folks call me Lucky."

Serena vaguely remembered a Lucky Doucet from high school. He'd been several classes ahead of her, an athlete, a loner with a reputation as a bad boy. The girls whose main interest in school had been guys had swooned at the mere mention of his name. Serena's interests had lain elsewhere.

She looked at him now and thought whatever reputation he had sown back then he had certainly cultivated since. He looked like the incarnation of the word *trouble*. She had to be half mad to even consider hiring him. But then she thought of Gifford. She had to see him, had to do what she could to find out what had made him leave Chanson du Terre, had to do her best to try to convince him to come home. As tough as Gifford Sheridan liked to pretend he was, he was still a seventy-eight-year-old man with a heart condition.

"I'm Serena Sheridan," she said in her most businesslike tone.

Lucky Doucet blinked at her. A muscle tensed, then loosened in his jaw. "I know who you are," he said, an oddly defensive note in his voice. Serena dismissed it as unimportant.

"I came here to hire a guide, Mr. Doucet. Gifford Sheridan is my grandfather. I need someone to take me out to his cabin. Mr. Gauthier has informed me that all the more reputable guides are booked up for the weekend, which apparently leaves you. Are you interested in the job or not?"

Lucky moved back to lean negligently against the counter again. Behind him, Lawrence had switched off his wrestling program in favor of live entertainment. In the background Iry LeJeune sang "La Jolie Blonde" in crackling French over the radio. *The pretty blonde.* How apropos. He took a deep pull on his cigarette, sucking the smoke into the very corners of his lungs, as if it might purge the feelings shaking loose and stirring inside him.

When he had stepped from the back room and seen her he had felt as if he'd taken a vicious blow to the solar plexus. *Shelby.* The shock had dredged up memories and emotions like mud and dead vines churning up from the bayou in the wake of an outboard motor—pain, hate, fear all swirling furiously inside him. The pain and hate were old companions. The fear was for the control he felt slipping, sliding through his grasp like a wet rope. The feelings assaulted him still, even though he told himself this wasn't the woman from his past, but her sister, someone he had never had any contact with. Nor did he want to. They were twins, after all, maybe not perfectly identical, but cut from the same cloth.

He stared at the woman before him, trying to set all personal feelings aside to concentrate on only the physical aspects of her. It shouldn't have been difficult to do; she was beautiful. From the immaculate state of her honey-colored hair in its smooth French twist to the tips of her beige pumps, she radiated class. There wasn't anything about her that shouldn't have been carved in alabaster and put in a museum. His gaze roamed over her face, an angel's face, with its delicate bone structure and liquid dark eyes—eyes that were presently flashing fire at him—and desire twisted inside him.

He swore, throwing his cigarette to the battered wood floor and grinding it out with the toe of his boot. Without looking, he reached behind the counter and pulled out a bottle of Jack Daniel's, helping himself to a generous swig. Lawrence said nothing, but frowned and glanced away, tilting his head in silent reproof. Resenting the twinge of guilt pinching him somewhere in the vicinity of where his conscience had once resided, Lucky put the bottle back.

Damn. He damned Gifford Sheridan for having grand-daughters that looked like heaven on earth. He damned women in general and himself in particular. If he had a lick of sense he would send Miss Serena packing. He would go about his own business and let the Sheridans do what they would.

That was the kind of life he had chosen to live, solitary, and yet other lives kept drifting into his. He didn't want to be touched. He didn't need the trouble he knew was brewing on the Sheridan plantation, Chanson du Terre, didn't need the reminder of past pain. But Giff had dragged him into it to a certain extent already and there was too much riding on the situation for him to decline playing so slight a role in the drama.

He cursed himself for caring. He had thought himself beyond it, thought the capacity to care had been burned out of him by the acidic quality of his experiences. But it was still there, which meant he had to find the strength to deal with it. God help him.

Serena gave him one last scathing glare and turned on her slim, expensive heel, heading for the street entrance of the store. Lucky swore under his breath and went after her, catching her by the arm.

"Where are you goin', sugar? I never said I wouldn't take you."

She looked pointedly at the big dirty hand circling her upper arm, then turned that defiant gaze up to his face. "Maybe *I* won't take *you*, Mr. Doucet."

"The way I see it, you don't have much of a choice. Ain't nobody else gonna take you out to Giff's." He laughed without humor. "Ain't nobody else crazy enough."

"But you are?"

He smiled like a crocodile and leaned down toward her until his mouth hovered only a few inches above the sweet tempta-tion of her lips. "That's right," he whispered. "I'm over the edge. I might do anything. Ask anyone 'round this town here. They'll all tell you the same thing—*Il n'a pas rien il va pas faire*. There's nothing he won't do. That Lucky Doucet, he's one bad crazy son, him."

"Well, I'm a psychologist," she said with a saccharine-sweet smile. "So we ought to get along just peachy, shouldn't we?"

He let go of her arm as if she had just told him she had leprosy. The expression of smug male arrogance abruptly disappeared, and his face became blank and unreadable. He turned and strode for a side door that stood open and led directly onto a dock.

Serena stood a moment, trying to gather some strength, her gaze on Lucky Doucet's broad bare back as he walked away. Her limbs felt like jelly and her stomach was quivering inside. She could feel old Lawrence staring at her, but she didn't move. She'd never had such a . . . primal reaction to a man. She was a sophisticated, educated woman, a woman who prided herself on her ability to maintain control in every situation. But that foundation of control was trembling in the wake of Lucky Doucet, and she didn't like it. He was rude and arrogant and . . . The other words that came to mind were far too flattering. What difference did it make what he looked like? He was a Neanderthal.

He was also her only hope of reaching Giff. And she had to reach him. Someone had to find out what was going on. Shelby claimed she hadn't a clue as to why Gifford had suddenly deserted the plantation in favor of living out in the swamp. It might have been nothing more than a matter of Giff getting fed up with having Shelby and her family underfoot while their new house was under construction, but it might have been something more. It wasn't like him to leave during a busy time of year, simply turning the reins of the sugarcane plantation over to his manager.

Shelby had peevishly suggested Gifford was getting senile. Serena couldn't imagine her grandfather as anything other than sharp as a tack, but then, she hadn't actually seen him in a while. Her practice in Charleston kept her too busy for many visits home. She had been looking forward to this one, looking forward to simply enjoying her ancestral home in all its springtime glory. Then Shelby had greeted her at the door with news of Gifford's defection to the swamp.

He'd been out there two weeks. Two weeks with no word, and Shelby had done nothing about it except complain.

"What did you expect me to do?" she had asked. "Go out there after him? I have two children to raise and a real estate business to manage and a husband, and I'm the chairperson of the Junior League drive for canned goods for the starving peasants of Guatemala. I have responsibilities, Serena! I can't just jump in a boat and go out there! Not that he would ever listen to a word I have to say anyway. And you can't expect Mason to go out there. You know how beastly Gifford is to him. I'm just at my wits' end trying to deal with him. You're the psychologist. You go out there and talk some sense into that hard head of his."

Go out there. Into the swamp. Serena's blood had run cold at the suggestion. It ran cold now at the thought. But she was just angry enough and stubborn enough to get past her fear for the moment. She had stormed from the house to go in search of a guide without even bothering to change her clothes. She wouldn't allow herself to dwell on her fear. She had to see her grandfather and there was only one way to do that. She had to go out into the one place she thought of as hell on earth, and the only man available to take her had just walked away.

Serena rushed after Lucky Doucet, struggling to hurry in her narrow skirt and shoes that had not been intended for walking on rough planking. The midday sun was blinding as she stepped out onto the dock. The stench of dirty water and gasoline hung in the thick, still air. Lucky stood at the open door to the workshop.

"We haven't discussed your fee," Serena said, ignoring the possibility that he had changed his mind about taking her. She struggled for an even breath as she faced his chest. Even up close he looked as if he were cast in bronze rather than flesh and bone.

He looked down his nose at her with an expression that suggested she had just insulted his mother. "I have no need of your money," he said contemptuously.

Serena rolled her eyes and lifted her hands in a gesture of exasperated surrender. "Pardon me for thinking you might like an honest wage for an honest job. How bourgeois of me."

He ignored her, bending to pick up a heavy cardboard box full of oily black motor parts. He lifted it as though it weighed no more than a kitten and set it on a workbench to sort through it. His attitude was one of dismissal and irritating in the extreme.

"Why are you making this so difficult?" Serena asked.

He turned his head and gave her a nasty, sardonic smile. "Because I'm a difficult kind of guy. I thought you might have figured that out by now. You're an intelligent woman."

"Frankly, I'm amazed you would credit a woman with having a brain. You strike me as the sort of man who sees women as being useful for only one purpose."

"I said you were intelligent, not useful. I won't know how useful you are until I have you naked beneath me."

Heat flared through Serena like a flash fire. She attributed it to anger. Certainly it had nothing to do with the sudden image of lying tangled in the sheets with this barbarian. She crossed her arms in front of her defensively and made a show of looking all around them before returning her belligerent gaze to Lucky. "Pardon me, I was just checking to see if I had somehow been transported back into the Stone Age. Are you proposing to hit me over the head with a dinosaur bone and drag me back to your cave, Conan?"

He raised a warning finger, his brows drawing together ominously over glittering eyes. "You got a mouth on you, *chère*."

He shuffled toward her, backing her up against the door frame. Serena managed to swallow her first gasp, but couldn't help the second one as his spread thighs brushed the outsides of hers. He braced his forearms on the wood above her head and leaned down close. His breath was warm against her cheek and scented with the smoky taint of tobacco and whiskey.

"I have *never* forced a woman," Lucky said, his voice low and soft, the molten gold of his eyes burning into Serena's. "I never have to."

He stared at her mouth with rapt fascination. It was rosy and soft-looking and he wanted badly to taste it, but he denied himself the luxury. She was a spoiled society bitch and he wanted nothing to do with her. He'd been burned badly enough to know better. *Dieu*, he'd learned his first lesson at the hands of her twin! To get that close again was to give in entirely to the demons of insanity.

Still, desire ribboned through him, as warm as a fever in his blood. The subtle, expensive scent of her perfume lured him closer. He dropped his head down near the curve of her shoulder and battled the urge to nuzzle the tender spot just below her ear and above the prim stand-up collar of her dark pink blouse. He could feel his sex growing warm and heavy.

"I'm hiring you as a guide," she said through her teeth, her voice trembling with rage or desire or both. "*Not* for stud service."

Lucky mentally thanked her for breaking the spell. He stepped back, cocking one hip and hooking a thumb in the waistband of his pants. He gave her a devilish grin. "Why not, angel? I'd give you the ride of your life."

She glared at him in utter disgust and walked away to stand at the edge of the dock, her slender back rigid. He had no doubt irreparably offended her ladylike sensibilities, he thought. Fine. That was exactly what he wanted. The more emotional distance he put between himself and a woman like Serena Sheridan, the better. His mother would have peeled the hide off him for talking that way to a woman, but this was more than just a matter of manners, it was a matter of survival.

He scooped up the box of motor parts and started down the pier with it, calling over his shoulder as he went. "So, you comin,' *chère*, or what? I don't have all day."

Serena turned and stared in disbelief as he headed down the worn dock. She noticed for the first time that his hair was nearly as long as hers, tied in a short queue at the back of his thick neck with a length of leather boot lace. A pirate. That was what he reminded her of—in looks *and* attitude.

"You're leaving *now*?" she said, once again rushing to catch up with him.

He didn't answer her. It was perfectly obvious he meant to leave. Serena cursed Lucky Doucet and spike heels in the same breath as she picked up her pace. Talk about your grade-A bastards, this guy took the prize. And she wanted to be the one to personally pin the medal on him, preferably directly onto that bare boilerplate chest of his. If they were in Charleston, never in a million years would she have put up with being treated the way he was treating her. She had too much sense and self-respect to fall for that tame-the-rogue-male syndrome, no matter how overwhelmingly sexy the rogue happened to be. But they weren't in Charleston. They were in South Louisiana, at the edge of the Atchafalaya Swamp, some of the wildest, most remote swampland in the United States. And Lucky Doucet wasn't some button-down executive or construction worker she could bring to heel with a cool look. He was a breed unto himself and only marginally more civilized than the bayou country around them.

Abruptly, the heel of one of her pumps caught between planks in the dock and gave way, nearly pitching Serena headfirst off the pier and into the oily water. She swore aloud as she stumbled awkwardly, hampered by the narrow skirt around her knees, just managing to catch her balance before it was too late.

Lucky stopped and turned toward her with a look of mock affront. "Why, Miz Serena, such language! What will the ladies at the Junior League think?"

She narrowed her eyes and snarled at him as she hopped on her ruined shoe and pulled the other one off. The instant she put her foot down, she ran a sliver into it, but she refused to cry out or even acknowledge the pain. She limped up to Lucky, struggling to maintain some semblance of dignity.

"I'm not prepared to leave just now, Mr. Doucet," she said primly. "I was thinking more along the lines of tomorrow morning."

He shrugged without the least show of concern. A brilliant white grin split his features. "Well, that's too bad, sugar, 'cause if you're leavin' with me, you're leavin' now."

FANFARE

On Sale in March

THE GOLDEN BARBARIAN

☐ (29604-3) $4.99/5.99 in Canada
by Iris Johansen

"Iris Johansen has penned an exciting tale. . . . The sizzling tension . . .is the stuff which leaves an indelible mark on the heart." --Romantic Times
"It's a remarkable tale you won't want to miss." --Rendezvous

MOTHERS

☐ (29565-9) $5.99/6.99 in Canada
by Gloria Goldreich

The compelling story of two women with deep maternal affection for and claim to the same child, and of the man who fathered that infant. An honest exploration of the passion for parenthood.

LUCKY'S LADY

☐ (29534-9) $4.99/5.99 in Canada
by Tami Hoag

"Brimming with dangerous intrigue and forbidden passion, this sultry tale of love . . . generates enough steam heat to fog up any reader's glasses."
--Romantic Times

TOUCHED BY THORNS

☐ (29812-7) $4.99/5.99 in Canada
by Susan Bowden

"A wonderfully crafted, panoramic tale sweeping from Yorkshire to Iceland . . . to . . .London. An imaginative tale that combines authenticity with a rich backdrop and a strong romance." -- Romantic Times

☐ Please send me the books I have checked above. I am enclosing $ _____ (add $2.50 to cover postage and handling). Send check or money order, no cash or C. O. D.'s please.

Mr./ Ms. _____

Address _____

City/ State/ Zip _____

Send order to: Bantam Books, Dept. FN, 414 East Golf Road, Des Plaines, IL 60016

Allow four to six weeks for delivery.

Prices and availability subject to change without notice.

THE SYMBOL OF GREAT WOMEN'S FICTION FROM BANTAM

Ask for these books at your local bookstore or use this page to order.

FN28 - 3/92

FANFARE

FANFARE

Sandra Brown

_____ 28951-9 TEXAS! LUCKY .... $4.50/5.50 in Canada
_____ 28990-X TEXAS! CHASE .... $4.99/5.99 in Canada

Amanda Quick

_____ 28932-2 SCANDAL .... $4.95/5.95 in Canada
_____ 28354-5 SEDUCTION .... $4.99/5.99 in Canada
_____ 28594-7 SURRENDER .... $4.50/5.50 in Canada

Nora Roberts

_____ 27283-7 BRAZEN VIRTUE .... $4.50/5.50 in Canada
_____ 29078-9 GENUINE LIES .... $4.99/5.99 in Canada
_____ 26461-3 HOT ICE .... $4.99/5.99 in Canada
_____ 28578-5 PUBLIC SECRETS .... $4.95/5.95 in Canada
_____ 26574-1 SACRED SINS .... $4.99/5.99 in Canada
_____ 27859-2 SWEET REVENGE .... $4.99/5.99 in Canada

Iris Johansen

_____ 28855-5 THE WIND DANCER .... $4.95/5.95 in Canada
_____ 29032-0 STORM WINDS .... $4.99/5.99 in Canada
_____ 29244-7 REAP THE WIND .... $4.99/5.99 in Canada

FANFARE

Rosanne Bittner

_____ 28599-8 EMBERS OF THE HEART . $4.50/5.50 in Canada

_____ 29033-9 IN THE SHADOW OF THE MOUNTAINS
$5.50/6.99 in Canada

_____ 28319-7 MONTANA WOMAN .... $4.50/5.50 in Canada

Dianne Edouard and Sandra Ware

_____ 28929-2 MORTAL SINS .... $4.99/5.99 in Canada

Tami Hoag

_____ 29053-3 MAGIC .... $3.99/4.99 in Canada

Kay Hooper

_____ 29256-0 THE MATCHMAKER, ... $4.50/5.50 in Canada

_____ 28953-5 STAR-CROSSED LOVERS .. $4.50/5.50 in Canada

Virginia Lynn

_____ 29257-9 CUTTER'S WOMAN, ... $4.50/4.50 in Canada

_____ 28622-6 RIVER'S DREAM, ... $3.95/4.95 in Canada

Beverly Byrne

_____ 28815-6 A LASTING FIRE .... $4.99/ 5.99 in Canada

_____ 28468-1 THE MORGAN WOMEN .. $4.95/ 5.95 in Canada

Patricia Potter

_____ 29069-X RAINBOW .... $4.99/ 5.99 in Canada

Deborah Smith

_____ 28759-1 THE BELOVED WOMAN ..$4.50/ 5.50 in Canada

_____ 29092-4 FOLLOW THE SUN .... $4.99/ 5.99 in Canada

_____ 29107-6 MIRACLE .... $4.50/ 5.50 in Canada

Ask for these titles at your bookstore or use this page to order.

Please send me the books I have checked above. I am enclosing $ _____ (please add
$2.50 to cover postage and handling). Send check or money order, no cash or C. O. D.'s
please.

Mr./ Ms. _____

Address _____

City/ State/ Zip _____

Send order to: Bantam Books, Dept. FN, 414 East Golf Road, Des Plaines, IL 60016
Please allow four to six weeks for delivery.

Prices and availablity subject to change without notice.   FN 17 - 12/91